Fey Ugokwe

WIFEY

Pink Purse International
Dallas

Published in the United States by Pink Purse International,
a division of Wharton King, LLC, Dallas.
www.pinkpurseinternational.net
Pink Purse International is a registered trademark of Wharton King, LLC.

ISBN: 978-0615764900

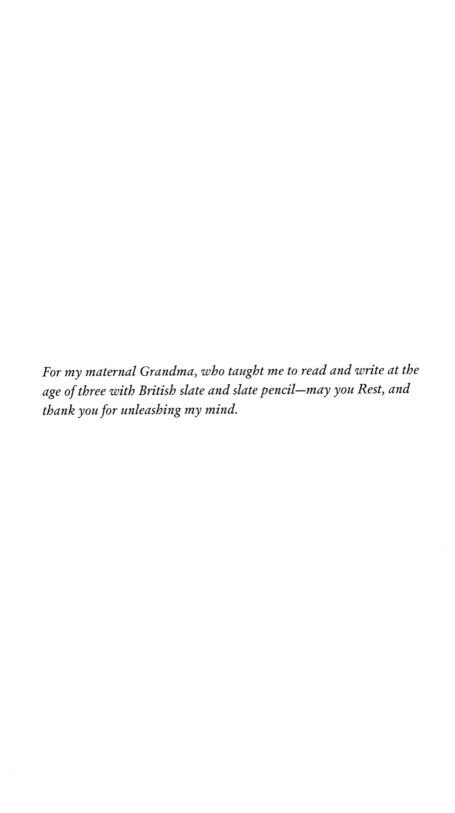

For my maternal Grandma, who taught me to read and write at the age of three with British slate and slate pencil—may you Rest, and thank you for unleashing my mind.

And their sounds were everywhere and jarring, a cackling din inescapable—so up, and so widely out—echoing their culture of meanings flat and plain across the fairways. And they, the instruments of sound, were all there assembled—as always, and by sure appointment—digging at plays from deep in the sear of the California sun, whooping and hooting once again at his crisply-told tales of her. They were abs so nonfat, flex, and concave unclinging to their blazing, old-school golf whites. They were big mouths full of bleach, organic chewing gum, and bonding, and bronze heads of kings thrown intermittently back from the zeal forces of a rocking good time. And hole after foundation-manicured hole, on the sprawl that was those public greens, they shot down pro balls, b.s., and the purported virtues of ex-girlfriends, fuck-friends, and would-be wives. So too, there, in the glint and sport, she of all peoples was re-christened by him 'Bourgie P'—the 'Bourgeoisie Princess'.

"*Naw, naw, naw,*" he would initially play at refusing, comically turning his back sharply, and scrunching a shoulder up and ear-ward—hand over mouth—in the pretense of girlish demureness and shyness. But at their routine of loudly protesting and dangerously swinging near the back of his head with 9 irons, he would launch quick-tongued and too eagerly into her latest offense:

"I mean, Boozhe P got ta eat *her* moo an' fries wit' a muh fuckin' knife an' fork! Y'heard? A muh fuckin' *knife an' fork* an' shit! For a muh fuckin' *burger*—not *even*—a trio a baby-ass *sliders* an' shit! Check dis out—Friday night, right? After da club, I took her ass ta dat new jazz spot dey be blowin' up on all da channels—"

"Yeah-yeah! I know dat place! Tha's *some* chicken an' waffles, man," one of his crew interjected. The rest too, in a doppler, murmured their agreement.

"Right? Dey *do* be puttin' dey foot *well up* into some down home, *for real.* Anyway, I was tryin' ta ease dat *fine, virgin ass* into some, you know, what yo' reverend might call *nighttime activities*, back at da ol' *Ebony Valley Lodge*…though on da real, despite da name, all ass is *accepted*—we don't *discriminate* up in dat mutha fucka!" They laughed out hard at his cultural twist on the reference, and at his general, coolly casual lawlessness— slapping each other in a brotherhood of knowingness at palms, fist bumping at big-school-ring-blinged knuckles.

"*Hahahahaha*—you ain' right, dawg! You ain't *riiight*," another player from his chorus piped in for the group, swinging at his head again. "Besides, you know *full well* dat's what dey call *my* house, ha-*ha*!"

"*Huh*," he replied, grinning. And then hand on heart, posing with an ankle crooked over foot, he reminded them, "Ya know what I always *say*, my bruthas—I may not be *right*, but I'm *real*."

"*Riiight, riiight*," the gallery in sound rounds concurred, still chuckling out to the fairways in echo.

"So, anyway—da shit was casual, right? So, we both order up dem sliders, right? An' sure if Miss Boozhe P didn' whip out doze silver-ass utensils from all up in dat napkin, yo—da *second* after she ordered dem shits. An' y'all know she asked f'dem *well done*, ta boot! An' *den*, she proceeded ta carve da muh fuckas up when dey came, like a muh fuckin' ninja ridin' horseback on a caravan a Christmas turkeys. I mean, *damn*. An' I had ta sit back an' *watch* all dat wannabe socialite shit—half da muh fuckin' night! It was all wrong, wrong, wrong. First of all, ya s'posed ta eat dem joints at least medium rare—e'en though dey mini—an' den jus' a let all a dem good juicy-juices just a *run down*. An' at *dat*, ya s'posed ta jus' a squish up all dat cheese, bread, an' fixins together, an' *wolf* dat sweet mess, in *one bite*—*two*, if you a *lady*. I mean, jus' like when we was kids—mouth aroun' as much a burger as you could fit in da fucka, an' dat's dat. *Shiiit.* Wasn' no knifery involved in dat shit!"

"*For real*—an' who was trus'in' us chil'rens back in da day wit' knives, anyway," one of them offered. "Muh fuckin' mess aroun' an' carve each other up half ta death an' shit." They all guffawed again, bending and flexing over athletically in boyish glee. They were whizzing off of a shared, man-felt invisible freeness, an ease, a silently privileged right. They were beautiful, accomplished, and effortlessly brilliant. And the all of it, their successes in 360, did not change by the words they used when together or by the way they sometimes lived their hours—and they knew that.

"Tell it. An' ta top it all off, after we lef' out, Boozhe P started playin' all Christmas coy wit' hers—so I didn' even get *some* a *none* a dem *sexy, spicy,* Trinidaddy goodies! I mean—got a brutha *all* wound up in da car. *Shiiit.* I mean, dere I was—doin' some *serious* dental work, all up in dat *juicy mouth* an' shit—an' you know, damn near performin' a muh fuckin' *tonsillectomy* on a sistah. An' she *let* me do dat shit—an' yet, wouldn' let me touch *nuthin*! No tit, no ass, no tat! *Shiiit.* I was holdin' onto da muh fuckin' car door for leverage an' shit, an' dat was da only thing a muh fucka *could* touch—an' it was *mine,* anyway! *Yo-yo-yo*—an' *den* she had da nerve ta e'en stop *dat* shit, *cold,* like a muh fucking crossing guard an' shit, an' ask me to drive her little ass home! *Shiiit.* Why I always git stuck wit' all da frou-frou, one-drop-a-black-blood havin', Comin'-to-America, blue-ballin', boozhe-ass bitches?"

"'Cause you *like* dem chicks, *man!*" another of his boys, arms wide, yelled up into the air, bending his neck backward to hurl out the sound. And each man in the crew nodded—some snickering—or nudged the man nearby knowingly.

The leader, frowning, picked up a loose ball and swung at it stylistic, whacking it hard despite the needless flourish, sending it air-sailing to a bounce clear beyond their natural view. "*Huh. Do* I?" he replied challengingly, just under his breath. But, despite their sometimes simultaneously buzzing smartphone texts, and voicemail alerts from irritated and foot-tapping girlfriends, wives, bosses, and partners, they all decidedly—amidst their own human and technological din—well heard him.

And then weeks later, against the inner misgivings racing chyme and its queasy thick up into the back of her throat, and the bells in her head all on and loud approaching—screeching their warnings at her—she allowed him to make both the margaritas and the mood. So, similarly thereafter, short for 'Bourgeoisie Princess', she was also dubbed 'Dat 'Ess'—as in "Boys, last night I was *all up in* Dat *'Ess!*"

And then one day, when they were finally, curiously, dubiously married, she was just 'Wifey' or 'Bourgie'—even to her face—yet still not her name, not ever her name.

She was a voluptuous 22 and stunning from Miami, nicknamed 'P.V.' for her first and middle initials, the daughter of affluent, conservative Trinidadians. She was a tan-skinned, unblemished, hair of ink and wavy falling to the shoulders, a petite-heighted goddess walking carefully among men. She fell hard for the concept of California, with all of its promise of continued sun and sea, coupled with its ideal of easy living—a concept her mother disdainfully termed 'The Freeness'. And when she was old enough to realize that the ticket out of her overprotective family's second home was college there, a life apart from their clench and on her own there, she glowed with an inner giddy, each newly unwrapping year.

But, her not-so-secrets upon leaving Miami were that she was quiet, shy, a virgin. She was fully a woman only in chronological numbers to most who knew her—and treated as such. As a child, she had been strictly trained in the ways of traditional, West Indian reticence, and of speaking when spoken unto—even in the face of fear, objection, anger. And so, given both her particular temperament and her rearing, she had learned well the inward pout and silent resistance, which formed and rose up, respectively, within her at needed instances—at simple whim. Yet, it was not that she only hailed from such dispositions. In actuality, her mother was idiosyncratically the reverse: she was feisty, outspoken and opinionated—brash if well-riled—whether speaking to her child, her husband, a friend, or whosoever the stranger else. But Nani—P.V.'s maternal grandmother—was the one that had truly shaped the child, in every interstitial space of her mechanism through the world. So, intellectually, P.V. embraced the liberated tongue and life-way of her mother, but in process, the antiquated deference and quiet defiance of her grandmother. And the latter way of being always took hold of her—at every time, it won out. Her mother was therefore worried for her, and begged her not to make the trip to California. She thought the state too big, vast, and fast for her daughter. But an impatience, a rebellious, marching insistence rose up within P.V. the year beforehand. And it made her use that rolling member in her mouth and stamp a foot down and hard, arms crossing in a tantrum for the sake of the big, unknown freedoms of which she had always dreamt. And so, with that as her gate opener, she was able to leave them—her parents and Miami—needing to get well out from under the Third World thumbs pressing in everywhere at her sense of true self. But she did so in a wake of reluctance and tears—inclusive of her, shocking, own.

And he at 25 was Rodney, a smooth, deep dark chocolate from end-to-end and glistening—a lean and towering native son orphaned at the age of four in the inner-skirts of Los Angeles. He was a one pulled up by his bootstraps—with the harshness of the world still heavy on his shoulders, and well-packed in layers embedded thick into his psyche. He was raised curiously by a smirking and rowdy, 18-year-old brother, and a paternal uncle who had a penchant for daily shooting back inordinate amounts of a 'medicinal' cocktail of cheap beer, discount cola, and blended Canadian whisky. But the two they still worked hard—as they played harder— teaching Rodney a gritty and responsible, steely-toiling social function, amidst utter domestic dysfunction. And he survived because of them, and moreover, in ambition, grew.

And Rodney loved his birthright L.A., knowing in his mind photographically every wondrous part of it, like each stretch of skin on a long-time girlfriend. In his short years, he had made a past-time of learning all of its secrets, haunts, and facets. He knew everything of the surrounding land mass, California, too—learning well even what to say both officially and unofficially about it to strangers passing through it. And each day, as pieces of his success flashed in the nonchalantly ascending sun—the sleek, metal frames of his expensive sunglasses; the heavy, high-end watch that dangled coolly from his bony wrist; and the slick finish on his new, luxury two-seater sports car—he blew well up within his chest with a quiet pride, to be making money over money in the land he had first entered into impoverished. He believed wholeheartedly that he had won at the game that sits on the necks of infants, rolling and bouncing at them—grinning, and trying to break them—upon their being born into starkness. As a result, he felt himself at the helm of California—at the bridge and the body, and not at the tail of it—with the other like-minded, battle-of-the- fittest others. He thought himself so specifically unlike those left perpetually, from the moment of their first breaths, in the state's economic tow. And, he felt that the ones who had made it, and those like him who had surmounted crises but were still climbing, had a responsibility to curtail the majority of their sweat equity to the state—to keep it running, smooth shining like gold, to stay in that marriage of person and land and calling.

But at the core of his soul, he felt left back by most of the people who shared his—jaw-drop shocking to some—newfound, reserved social politic; take on life; view of the widening world. So, together and viscous with the dark of what had already been poured into him as a boy, all sat not so well with him. And unbeknownst to him, that all had already begun to corrode, eating swiftly and cleanly away at, his insides.

And so they were. And together, as a newly married couple, they immediately replaced their separate, one-bedroom apartment lives with the sizeable purchase of a Spanish-style, four-bedroom house. And their twelve sorority bridesmaids and twelve frat groomsmen, together with an utterly disinterested, bred poodle named Rome, were permanently always as buffers between them. They had no need to learn one another, as their living weekdays were dutifully spent each working at their separate mills, with the weeknights and weekends simply flowing back and forth between friends and clubs and each other and everything else—just as things were before they were married. So, everything betwixt them at every hour was easy as college, with a demonstrably better roommate situation.

Sexually, for her part, P.V. didn't pretend to understand the all and all of what Rodney did to her at night, nor did he bother to explain it to her. And, for Rodney's part, there was decidedly an unfurling list of darker things that he wanted done—and to do—which, per his expectations, she dutifully obliged him. Each time however, P.V. heard, felt, objections to his roughening wants, bleating 'no's' silently out to her from the core of her conscience. In their universe outside of bed, Rodney also cranked up the intensity of his juvenile teasing of her, kicking it up to the next several levels. And he became a one slipping his ribbing of her, skillfully, into the majority of the conversations within their marital waters, like a good hand at cooking salt. His quick, quipping tongue—though always sheathed in the light-hearted—was strategically aimed now to jiggle her overall foundation, to cause an unsteadiness and insecurity within her, to explore and test her boundaries and limitations. And he was so good at it—at both perceiving and gleaning her fears, faults, vulnerabilities. And he was taking tally and memo of them, storing them away in the grey of his brain, for whenever that rainy day to hurl them against her was to come.

It was the money between them that was truly their sure and swell. And it sprang forth abundantly, in clear waters—forces powered by their sweat equities, and the support of reasonable times. Increasingly, Rodney's extras began to be spent on elaborate boys' weekends away in Las Vegas with his groomsmen-and-other-cronies crew—taking in strip shows at higher and higher-end gentlemen's clubs; golfing ever-increasingly pristine greens; and exploring the limits of personal training, metrosexual massages, and men's couture shopping. He thought nothing of any of it, assigning to it all a right that he had as a free, working, industrious, and ambitious young man. Before long, he had purchased for himself a spank-shiny, new black Harley—though he had never previously ridden a motorcycle—and additionally, to keep up with some of the more stunt-oriented members of his crew, a bright red, Japanese-make racing bike. So, on the weekends before setting sail for Las Vegas with his boys, Rodney was—down to the hour—white shirt flying up, ruffling in the wind; a long, smooth black back arching forward; a body leaning in and out of lanes without conscience. He was, in those moments before departure, a big free boy forever. But inside, he was a case study in the science of being careful of what is poured into children, the wee ones of the world whose grey-matter molds are *de facto*, not yet cooled. For he had seen things done, and heard about done things, in the corners of his youth and rising—done and things that were not good things. And as a result of his particular mind's own sorting of them, despite all seemings, he was completely not thought- or soul-well.

P.V.'s leavings were put toward spot cooking classes and winery tours with her fellow sorors, and other events of a cultured-living ilk. She fancied herself neither talented nor creative enough to actually approach enrollment in a school for that which was the chief of her interests—all things culinary—and so was willing to merely stay at the feet of it, approaching it inch by inch with a multitude of interruptions. In those hours of a learning and a tasting here and there, alongside her endless circles of effusively giggling, chattering friends, she simply felt like a big girl shaping up adult interests—growing, spiraling up—all in a slow and beaming, comfortably-paced time.

But it wasn't always a study of jamming intersections betwixt the young wife and husband. Sometimes the entirety of their world was completely well—when Rodney occasionally permitted himself to relax to a purer version, causing the sweeter, big-teenaged rays encapsulated deeply within to radiate well and out.

"*Ooooh, Wifey,*" he cooed one day, folding his wingspan-like arms around her shoulders and backwards, tugging teasingly at the bow-tied strings of her couture, floral halter. "Um, since you been takin' all doze cooking classes, maybe you could whip us up a batch a gourmet whipped cream, an'..." he paused and raised his eyebrows suggestively in rapid succession, mouth open in an animated grin.

P.V. giggled, blushing profusely, and offered, "Um…I'm like, not there yet with like, *dessert toppings* and stuff, but um…I don't know—maybe we could like…just get the stuff in the canister?"

"No—*freshhhh,*" Rodney replied quickly, raising an index finger, his exaggerated smile widening deeper into the same ridiculous expression. "Girl, I'm gon' *be* fresh, so I *wants* it fresh—I *needs* it fresh!" P.V. giggled out hard in appreciative response, always at a desire for Rodney's playfulness, lightness, his big-kid funny. "Besides, a brutha got a hangover ta-day, so I don't need it to be makin' dat whippit sound when we gittin' down—*shrrr*? *Shrrr*? *Naw.* Ain't no headache medicine for dat. No, serious—dat's what it sound like ta me. Like somebody startin' a car an' askin' a question at da same damn time. Downright *distractin'* to a brutha!" And, encircling her waist with his elegant, stretching palms and fingers, he drew her up close to him. Gazing down and into her mischievously as her body convulsed with giggles, he gauged her reaction carefully, clinically—and again, mentally recorded and neatly, stored it.

On another day, deep in a booth in their new fave restaurant, Rodney leaned across the table, eyes widened, lips pursed, eyebrows raised in mock shock. "*Wifey*," he whispered strenuously, playfully—reaching out to gently tap P.V.'s arm in an almost feminine fashion, and turning up his lips over a loopy smile. He was staring at her as if covertly—head turned slightly in one direction, sight shifted over at her in the other—like a BFF with a big secret.

"Ah?" she replied distractedly, glancing up just in time to catch his hilarious expression.

Rodney chuckled in response amidst his routine, relaxing and remarking aloud in his normal, earthy baritone, "You *still* catch me off guard wit' dat mess—'ah?' *Hahahahahahaha*—you so cute wit' yo' *fine, Trinidadian ass*, Wifey."

P.V. tittered, and lowered her head again. She slid her spoon into the bright green gazpacho, at an angle away from her, and scooping some up, rested it neatly on the outer lip of the bowl. Tilting the spoon toward her slightly, she leaned over, and eagerly began studying its contents—engrossed in the magic and consistency of the soup. To her, it all looked like lumps of jeweled water-ice winking, and she was little-big-girl entranced by it. Rodney watched her intently, wavering somewhere between amusement and intrigue.

"*Wifey*," he whispered urgently, jocularly again. P.V. smiled up at him, and then lowering her head yet again, returned to perusing the contents of her soup.

"*Wifey,*" Rodney whispered a third time.

P.V. uttered a quiet, repressed wave of giggles again, and looked up and into him. "Yeah?"

Rodney leaned forward, glancing exaggeratedly to and fro, as if to see who was listening. And then, half-rising and stretching his torso fully across the table, he whispered into P.V.'s ear: "*Wifey—I 'on't know who da chef is, but man or woman, I'm a bounce back dere an' kiss dem straight up in dey mouth. 'Cause dis right here's off da chain, Wifey. 'ts good.*" P.V., despite herself in the surroundings, birthed out a quick series of loud laughs that rolled into the ambience. Then she crinkled up her tiny nose as her chest continued to heave—looking at him sideways, eyes squinting in feigned disgust.

"*Seriously,* Wifey," Rodney continued breathily, returning to his seat. Closing his eyes, he hunched his shoulders up, arms wrapped around himself in a mock embrace, and rapidly pouted his thick lips up again to kiss the air. "*Mwaaahhh!*" he cried out with a simper. P.V. was laughing so hard that tears had begun to form around her eyes. Reaching out, she swatted half-admonishingly at one of his long, smooth—and profoundly muscular—arms.

It was like that—all of the time. So, together with the money from their industries spent on their new young lives together, they swam effortlessly through the days and nights, toward infinity. And they reveled in it—he more than she—in all the things and people and experiences made of the summery gloss of almost superlatively blessed, young beingness. Somewhere, too, at the edges of their consciousnesses, they fully expected to have the room to make their running-forward mistakes, to learn, to grow up into being whatever they were to be individually. And equally, they expected to mature together into whatever that unionized thing was that they had strapped themselves too quick into, that endless, thick-fog ride that was the truly being married.

But then one day, unexpectedly, the sun rose sweepingly black upon the state—and it wasn't the only one—and they awoke to find themselves holding onto nothing but what was standing in three dimensions, and what little they had jointly saved. They had eagerly spent—as if single college co-eds—without much store-housing, always encouraged by the reality that together, they could easily generate sufficient and more. So, in the fresh darkness, their carefree, economic togetherness began to crack, splinter, web. It all started when on a Monday, Rodney's bosses assigned him to train a new marketing team member from their New York office, and then summarily that Friday, swiftly laid him—and his entire marketing unit—off, except for the one employee he had been forced to mentor. The fragmenting downspiral continued with P.V. realizing that the once flock of eager, wild-eyed buyers had run, scattering well deep, into hiding. Accordingly, she helplessly—an additionally, inexperienced one—watched as her real estate-for-sale listings inventory rolled and aging sat, month after nail-biting month. Resultantly, for income, the two began to snatch away anxiously at the rest of their dwindling, pea-sized savings, and at the vapors of P.V.'s plummeting realtor commissions.

Suddenly, the two together were thinking older, living older—too much older than their individual years. They began redefining the meaning of frills, and withholding those like penny-pinching pensioners, things they once thought of as basics, that they used to, in better times, allow themselves without blinking. And so, they were struggling to maintain no longer the burgeoning, middle income luxe that they had begun to build, but dearly, just the very safe that they had at least, once been. Yet, somehow, the very last to be redefined—to go—were Rodney's expensive man-crew weekends away to revel, and the first to be jettisoned, long before the redefining, P.V.'s buffering girlfriend trips to cook and soothingly dine. And then one day, in the choking grit and dust wake of it all, for the first time—inclusive of the days of their respective singlehoods—they were broke, miserable, and officially stuck with someone. They were left id-minded, like runaway children caught up in a typhoon at blind-side—force-dragged into an undertowing cycle downward and downward still, eyes squeezed shut intermittently and little arms looped, each round the other's, league by league in the under together.

Rodney awoke with a jolting, eyes-up-open-in-a-flash, start. It was as if a hypnotist had bid him loudly, firmly to wake up—snapping fingers together with an equal harsh force, to facilitate his return to full reason. His eyes were the only part of him that first moved, and he let them do the work as he lay there—rest of body static—by increments perceiving, breathing in the morn. Yellow-white rays of California sun were just beginning to stream slightly in through the luxe, half-slanted open, teal linen blinds. They shifted to illuminate too, the lower tips of the matching, clean-lines-contemporary window treatments that neatly boxed both windows. At an angle out like a tipping domino, the elongated shadow of the window loomed on the pristine—and real—white oak floorboards. Rodney twisted slightly to ease a twinge of pain, the minor injury a result of having slipped and almost fallen the night before, on the pristine, white and grey marble tiles that paved his and P.V.'s master bathroom. P.V. was a heavy head to his chest, her mass of black, medium-length, hot-curled hair almost neatly contained in the crook of his elbow. She was still breathing in the realm of sleep, but her little body was tossing and gesturing at intervals, as if walking and acting in that unseen world. And at that very moment, in fact, forever unbeknownst to him, P.V. was indeed dreaming—of Nani.

In the dream, Nani appeared physically as her normal self: she was a beautiful—almost brown—bent-forward-midway-at-the-waist and thin, but wide-bodied, woman. Her parabolic bearing always made her seem as if she were perpetually giving *salaam*, a condition caused by her incorrigibly poor posture as a girl, and the late stages of osteoporosis in her end years. Her smooth, black hair was parted in the middle, and streaked with coarser, fly-away strands of white, all disappearing into a long braid that peeked out again near her waist. She was standing in Trinidad, outside P.V.'s parent's first home together, in an alcove portion off the veranda that was sheltered by the low, Spanish-tiled roof of the house. In the distance, P.V. could see the blanched sands of the beach, and the sparkling, green-blue waters rolling and retreating on its thin lip. But Nani was oddly barefoot—and alarmingly sheathed from top to bottom in a white sheet that was wound about her body in sections, as if on a mummy. She was muttering and curved over a roti flat pan and board, spindly fingers slightly floured and glistening from the oil mix. One roti was already sizzling on the flat pan, and to her left, there was a large, white china plate with a royal blue pattern, heaped high with all that she had previously cooked.

The sky suddenly darkened into a night, with a large, spinning patch of daylight in the distance—and bright, rich, almost blindingly deep-blue flowers began to fall out of the air to everywhere. The blooms, each as if clovers springing out their vivid blossoms from a single stalk, dropped on top of Nani's head and onto her shoulders, immediately bouncing off on impact to the area around her. And they fell onto the food and preparation table, sticking into the mixing bowl containing the remainder dough, and blanketed the entire surface of the ground and tiled veranda floor. One huge stalk fell violently and lodged behind Nani's ear, its tip caught in her hooped, gold earring.

And Nani seemed to abruptly become aware of P.V's presence—whipping about sideways to face her, straightening completely up from the waist as would have been impossible for her, braid jerking to and fro with the immediacy of the motion. In her right hand was the stack of roti, topped with the new roti that had been in the pan—which was still gleaming—a flaky, beckoning nourishment, slightly charred and golden in spots. And grunting, face ashen and gaunt, she extended the breads to P.V., wrinkled right hand shaking out an urgency for her to take them. But when P.V. reached for that right hand, Nani moaned and extended her left, which—flesh inexplicably missing in parts—began to gush a dark red blood, thick from the palm and up over like discovered crude oil, from deep within its center. Below Nani's abdomen, from well within the white sheets that swaddled her entire body, blood began to gush thickly through—from her skin underneath up to the front of the sheets. The blood rapidly seeped and spread in a defined, enlarging 'v' shape from everywhere outside of her vagina, and similarly began springing as a pooling whole from each of her breasts. Turning slowly, back to P.V., she revealed that the blood too, was overtaking the sheets down in a long line, from the split of her buttocks, to the area near her rectum. Nani pivoted again in a flash, the white sheets almost entirely covered in the seeping out red. Her mouth was louder moaning, facial features knit together in excruciating pain, her left hand still outstretched and balancing the bottomless fountain of blood.

P.V. screamed—a long, loud, slow thing surreally caught by the dream air and then muted, rendered a nothingness in that portal of Time. She felt herself still screaming and wailing in her sleep, waves of aching grief pounding from the middle of her chest into her throat and bearing out through her mouth. But, she heard none of her own sounds in the dream. She reached out to try and clamp the blood fountaining from Nani's hand, and instantly awoke that way—hands outstretched, face streaming tears, neck straining forcefully out in silent moans.

"*Wifey, Wifey, Wifey,*" Rodney said low and firmly, shaking her awake into his embrace. "*Girrrl*—what's *up*? What's *up*, huh? Where you *at*, where you *at*—what you *dreamin'*?" P.V. opened her eyes and gazed up against Rodney's chest to see his head cocked to one side, brown eyes intently staring down into her. She lowered her head again, looking blankly out at the wall. "*Wow*, girl," he sighed, hugging her head and shoulders into him further. They were quiet for awhile, the only sounds those of the soft crash of waves in the distance, and the long, squeaking call of seagulls. She started to drift off again to sleep, comforted by the strength of his hold, but Rodney, head already swirling from the previous weeks, months, years, could not let the moments stay still.

"Rollin' blackouts, wil'fires, drought, housing crash, muh fuckin' layoffs—*an'* can't find no job? *Shiii*—I know *two* mutha fuckas tha's gittin' da *fuck* outta Cali!" he exclaimed, both to her and to the ceiling. "*Shiii*—it's like da mutha fuckin' *end a days* up in here! A brutha already had to deal wit' earthquakes, mudslides, an' wil'fires—e'en got used ta da rollin' blackouts back when an' shit. But a brutha *tired* an' shit, now. I mean—an' now all *dis* shit? Ain' time ta be workin' apparently—time ta be fuckin' *laid off* an' shit? *Naw, naw, naw*—*Rodney* don't *play dat* shit. Dis shit *absolutely*, muh fuckin' *ridiculous*." Lungs temporarily drained of their ire, Rodney kissed the top of P.V.'s head, which was still cradled gently in the nook of his elbow. And then, rolling over, he summarily made love to her. But P.V. was not present—and he did not seem to be aware of it. Her mind was still wrapped up in the fright of the dream of Nani, inner eyes gazing in horror at the blood shooting up and out from Nani's palm. During and after the sex, she cried—piteously, inconsolably—body shuddering in deep sobs from the lungs, seemingly emptying her whole head of water onto Rodney's skin. "It's *alright*. It's *alright*, *Wifey*," Rodney breathed. "Any year wit' a eight in it *bound* ta be good, *regardless*. I mean—layin' down, eight's da symbol for Infinity, right? An' Infinity is mutha fuckin' *limitless*, right? So, it's gonna be a *good* year. *Our* year. A year wit'out *limits*."

It was early in the month of All Hallows, and she had never been to Texas before. As the plane roared into its initial descent, she lifted the window shade and glimpsed the widespread of it through the scratched, oval pane. It was tract after tract after tract of flat, boxy, brown land, the green desiccated largely out of it by an everywhere and white-hot, relentless sun. Nearer still, and she could discern a better view of the almost camouflaged sand-and-land-colored houses, and equally hued, commercial buildings. She drew back abruptly, yanking the shade down—her spirit, at once, irritated. She looked around nervously, but thankfully, there was none to complain about the sudden absence of bright light: the passenger next to her was still deep-sleeping, and the one on the aisle avidly engaged in conversation with his companion across it. After a few moments, she felt the scenery beckoning to her again, and re-raising the shade, she instinctively whipped out her smartphone and captured whatever was passing by, on still. She sighed as her thumb slid at the new entries in her photo gallery, her irk reducing down to a low-grade depression. The images were nothing compared to descending in over L.A., Miami, or Trinidad to her: the place seemed so devoid of hue, variation, intrigue, life. It was as if something blazing had come and scorched over a neatly drawn architect's rendering, somehow declaring a perfection over the result.

P.V. was already upset with Rodney for determining, insisting, that they essentially needed to try to outrun recession—that they needed to leave the ocean-lapped, crayons-in-64-vivid state that she liked and he loved, for the dry and sprawling *this*, now housed unceremoniously in her phone's pic gallery. And she was seething that the *this* Rodney had so blindingly consigned first to *her*—with its unknown-to-both-of-them-ness; its seeming bland; and its route air hostesses full of big hair, big teeth, big laughs, big bling—so naturally extra giddy and drawling as they re-anchored at their home port again. It seemed, comparatively, all too much of a not-for-her in the quiet, little ego and blue of a mood into which she had so profoundly sunken.

And—there was something else. Her mum had always told her that one never realized the price of freeness until it was almost surely gone. She felt that now—the heavy anvil of truth behind that offhand-given, West Indian-ized wisdom. For her in the instant days, a nagging, whispering thing about being *told* by Rodney that they were moving, kept tapping at, not sitting well in the swallow with, her. Their dating life had actually not been like that—it had been full of "what you wanna do?", and "'t's up to you, Boozhe", and the like. Inasmuch as those days were in and of themselves curious—a set of a new strange that she was beginning to realize should not have led to marriage, she nevertheless started to miss them. So, somewhere at the edge of her, she frequently began to hearken well back, to the times of her singledom with him—to those easier, breathable, unentangled series of hours. And as she rose with everyone on the plane—amidst the unsettled symphony of bag zipping, chatter, briefcase clasp snapping, laughter, and overhead bin latch creaking—she wanted someone urgently to tell her if having ridden this craft to an unknown at her husband's behest was indeed what wivery was truly supposed to be.

When she stepped out onto the pavement, suitcase wheels making that familiar sound of a million marbles rolling behind her, the sun flashed hard like lightning onto P.V.'s skin. Her brain immediately complained, *too bright too bright no filter.* The strong rays were a blinding white bouncing wide off the pavement cement and everywhere, and then back up, full-on into smarting eyes again. Even the air of itself was oppressive—hot, and sticky-muggy from a recent rain. But, as the overly air-conditioned taxi that picked her up smoothed forward—past the long, stretching limits of the airport—she was shocked at what she saw. There were highways futuristic, looping around and over each other, an unbelievably track-upon-track-upon-track—like a living child's racing set—careening all the way up to a beautiful, boundless, light-blue sky. And equally, her eyes spanned across and caught glimpses of the large expanses of surprisingly hilly greens that lined the freeway underpasses like astroturf. But then, too, in an instant—she saw them. Whizzing past the fully-closed taxi window were the eerie, purple-blue flowers that had coated Nani—and everywhere—in her parent's Trinidad, in her dream. She was jolted to a fright by the very sight of them, an unsteady feeling quickening across her head, heart, core. Her mind began replaying her nightmare in quick scene succession, searching frantically for the hidden meanings. All the while, there were people—likely tourists—who had disembarked from their vehicles on the shoulder of the interstate, wading amongst the stalky blooms, examining and taking pictures with them. She watched at all of it as the taxi jostled past, with a sickening, heart-dropping awe.

Hands shaking, P.V. rummaged through her purse for the small tin of mints that, previously starving, she had purchased back in the airport. It was a white metal box with the state of Texas topography etched colorfully into the entirety of the top lid. She opened it at the corner like Rodney would, letting some of the sweets slide beyond its inner wax paper and directly into her mouth. The unusual taste of rose and soap with a back-kick of eucalyptus greeted her tongue, wrapped in an equally curious last-layered hint of potpourri. They weren't the strong-punching, clearly peppermint English mints that her mum always mailed off to her in alarming quantities—that she was secretly, slightly addicted to—but they were somehow altogether intriguing and oddly comforting, and achieved the aim of lulling her anxiety down to a quiet.

Later, she joined Rodney on video chat from her laptop, in her budget-friendly, Arlington inn room. It was going to be a ridiculously busy day, with a blitz of a meeting over lunch with a local realtor, and then off with the same on a harried hunt for a place to rent, store, exist.

"Now remember, Wifey," Rodney warned, switching sharply into a parental tone, "we on a budget, so don' go gittin' boozhe on da crib, y'feel me?" His head was almost humorously looming back and forth, long and oval in the laptop screen—a top-heavy, dark geometry against the pastel backdrop of their unlit bedroom. He was wearing a grey fleece hoodie that still bore the sweat stamps from his jog earlier. And he was persistently days unshaven, his moustache, connecting beard, and sideburns seemingly more thickly growing into a jet black and woolly than they even had in the wee hours of that morning.

P.V. wanted to laugh out loud at the misshapen sight of his head floating back and forth onscreen—like a great big balloon—but her inner child gave way to an adult grimace at his condescending, instructive inflection. The discomfort of being *told to do*, for the umpteenth time since he had unilaterally made the decision to relocate, returned to well up hotly in her gut against him. "Okay." she replied shortly, quietly—lips pressing in, teeth rapidly setting straight and firmly on themselves. In restraining her mouth so abruptly, she accidentally bit the tip of her tongue, and the attendant, warm, salty ooze of blood began filling the left side of her mouth. She sat hard back in the chair, petulantly adjusting the volume down on the laptop.

"I mean, *you* da realtor, so like I *said*—bettah *you* dan *me* doin' this right now," Rodney contended, stuffing his hands into the front pockets of his hoodie. "An' besides—ya *know* I hate house huntin', from da *las'* time we did it up *here*. Ya *know* I'd rather be on da links, or goin' to da game, or even gittin' my fuckin' man-mani on. Lookin' for cribs jus' puts a brutha off a day *entirely*, an' ya *know* this."

P.V., now fully peeved, nodded once without meaning it, gaze well away from the screen. But in the next moment, able to bear it no longer, she grabbed up her purse, half-rising from the chair—finger on the laptop button to power all of Rodney's madness down. "Um, I've got to go," she mumbled. "Like, Juanita's going to be knocking soon."

"Wifey." Rodney's tone was flat. Taking his hands out of his pockets, he propped up his elbows on their platinum-colored, metal swivel chair, and placed one hand on top of the other, to form a loose fist. "We *married* now, an' you don't jus' get ta do what *you* wanna do. *Now*, you got a *husband* to conten' wit'—an' you gon' ha' to *adjust* to dat shit." But P.V. replied nothing, her West Indianness—Nani-style—bidding her to continue to bear down, bite down. She reluctantly lowered herself back into the chair, hands still tight about the handles of her purse.

"*Boozhe*," Rodney insisted, leaning into the webcam, voice squeaking and crackling with reception interruptions at intervals. "Look. I *luh* Cali. I luh it like a woman. And unlike *you*, I'm actually *from* here. Remember dat shit, because dat shit is highly muh fuckin' *relevant*. What *dat* shit means is dat I ain' jus' gon' *leave* a place I *love*—an' am from—jus' all willy-nilly an' shit. I'm a *man*. I been *through* it wit' Cali—an' stayed—an' dat's how it is wit' good family. You don' jus' *run* from good *family*. But all dis here particular economic bullshit is *highly unprecedented*—an' you of all people in yo' business should *know*, an' *respect*, dat. You should be fuckin' on *my* side about all dis shit. So, if *I'm* sayin' we got to go, is 'cause I feel like shit has so *dramatically changed*, ta where we don' really have a choice. An' I'm sayin'—like I done *told* you, *so many times* on dis issue—*we don't*. We *don't* have a choice. An' I *know* dis shit is gittin' everywhere now, but like I said, dey say it's a little bettah in Texas an' places like dat—cost a livin' an' *all* dat

related shit. So *I* say—*ag'in*—den dat's where we got to *be* right now. *Period.*
I mean—we *young* an' shit. Dis is what we *should* be doin'—rollin' da dice
an' takin' a risk when shit go south—'cause we fuckin' *can*. I mean, I'm a git
a job dere—I know a couple dudes dere. An' you already applied for yo'
license ta practice down dere—so it's already *done*. Seriously, Wifey—you
actin' like we *ninety* an' shit." Filling his cheeks with air, he dismissively
blew his lips together, shaking his head. "Anyway—I sold off some a da
big shit already—da 'cycles, and some a da equipment, da skis, *blah blah blah
blah blah*. An' most a da rest of *dat* stuff I put online ta sell. Got rid a da
dog—found some dude an' his wife on a online ad site who wanted it. Dis
for real, Wifey—ain' no go-backs. So you best git *wit'* it—*quick*."

P.V. was still rigid in the standard, hard-upholstered inn room desk
chair throughout Rodney's tirade, pissed and unconvinced, the discomfort
at being preached to transforming into an extreme distaste for the person
she had married. And she wondered in the next instant why she *had*
married him—it seemed silly now. She had bartered away her freedom,
because of whatever she in a daze did back then, when she was younger,
needier, more up walking like a love-struck teenager in the clouds.
She began wishing back completely nostalgic, wishing she could click heels
in her head and return to being single and unattached just then—so that
she could wholly reclaim Cali, or hop a flight to Miami, or escape, better
desperately yet, to Trini. She sighed as well, idly fiddling with the computer
keys. She still couldn't believe they were married, and now they were here
in this moment doing all of this. There had been no adjustment time, no
downtime, no alignment period—nothing like that. They had gone from
weird whirlwind to party, to it being like cozy college roomies. And now in
a flash, everything had streaked well beyond that—and it was all too real,
different, fast. It was as if her BFF had become her daddy, and *he* didn't
even take on with her like that. She looked into the screen again, and

rapidly looked away, feeling that she had just glimpsed too much of a face in pixel that she could do well without at the moment.

Rodney arched further forward into the webcam, such as to deliberately distort the view of his face—partly for comic effect, and partly, somewhere in his careful, always conscious-and-watching psyche, to drive the nail in on his point. "*Yo*," he said, at almost point blank in the screen, forehead and rest of features appearing bulbous and dented at angles, as, straight-faced, he profiled swiftly then held it in still, from side to side. Then he leaned further in, head back completely. All P.V. could see was nose. "I know I'm probably gon' be bawlin' like a infant all da way on da drive down dere, Wifey. Like a *infant*, Wifey. *Aaahh—waaahh*. Like a lil' *bitch*. An' you *know* m'boys gon' give me *much* flack for dat. *Much* a da flackness. I mean, look at dis nose—see all up in here? *Aaahh*—look at it, Wifey! *Aaahh*. It gon' be all snotty and runnin' in a few days behind all dis shit, Wifey—look! *Aaahh—waahh*, Wifey! *Aaahh—waaahh!*"

But somehow, Rodney wasn't quite as breezily funny as he used to be. There was a decided strain and hard edge to his humor, and P.V. moreover, wasn't in the mood for laughing. Her whole California world was continuing to recede from her with each sand-slipping, Texas moment, and she was on end about it in her soul. She realized that somewhere, she wanted Rodney to say that as his wife, she had an equal vote in where they ended up—and that if she really objected to it, even at such a late stage, things could still be reversed, changed. Onscreen, she was a study in ice— face set hard in profile, eyes fixed at an imaginary point off to one side, lips drawn back and down. She waited—a seething statue, a being hardly breathing.

Rodney sat back, a tad surprised, amused, and irritated that his attempt at comedy had—for once—fallen flat on P.V., had not eased her back in line. And he made a mental note of it, for later. Things were already changing as rapidly as their finances had—and apparently, so was she.

"Uh-*huh*. Okay, okay—have it *yo'* way an' shit, Wifey," he said gruffly, flipping his sweatshirt hood up onto his head, and drawing the strings—in one hand's pull—tight. "You know wha's up? You already negotiated da lease on our house, right? 'Cause I said we needed tenants, so we could still pay dis mutha fuckin' mortgage ta try to keep dis shit, right? Well—I jus' got dat lease back signed, ta-*day*. An' you know what else is up, Wifey? Jus' like I *said*, me an' all twelve a m'boys gon' be drivin' *my* Jeep an' *yo'* fuckin' *boozhe-ass convertible* down dere in a matter a days—in a matter a *days*, Wifey." He shoved his hands into his hoodie pockets, flexing his shoulders in for effect. "An' what we cain't pack into dem cars for da road gon' be followin' me by mail in a few days after *dat*. So unless you wanna deal wit' *me* arrivin' ta no *address*, and da rest of our shit goin' ta charity by postal happenstance, you *best* git us a place *quick*—realtor dat yo' ass *is*, an' shit. An' it *best* be somethin' reasonable, an' non-*boozhe-ass*, for us an' all our stuff to be up *in*, at *dat*. So, you know wha's up, Wifey? *Huh*? I'm tellin' you—*dat's* wha's *up*."

P.V. turned her head back to the screen, in time to catch Rodney's dark stare-down—his eyes steady and glowering in the grey of the background, meaning everything reflecting within them. The realization popped up again, circling around and around on levels within her, alerting her to the fact that he had become in a few moons someone with which she was—and likely had always been—ill-equipped to deal. He was perhaps too much for her, too advanced. And she wondered how she had elbowed out a true awareness of that at each and every juncture, from dating through the very day of their wedding, and well beyond.

It occurred to P.V. too, that a portion of the stew of displeasure and resentment simmering within her originated from being, feeling, isolated—

of having been severed from her ring of California friends, her wondrously makeshift, vibrant, adopted family, by Rodney's decision and none of her own. Because of all of the activity that flowed from their impending move, she had been unable to truly consort with her girlfriends—or even her mother—about his conduct, words, mood, unilateral mandate. It had all called for a Thursday-through-Saturday girl's weekend away with her bridesmaids, over an animated roundtable of advice. It almost literally begged for that wined-up women's session, where hilarious and risqué novelty wine glasses also had their say—as did the red varietals brimming them, with their equally alluring and snappy monikers. And it pleaded too, for a protracted cell phone call to Miami, whilst luxuriating over a light afternoon tea at her fave teahouse—the fragrant, bergamot brew swirling in a whimsical and shiny china—as she lent her ear to her mum's pickling-salted view of her marital situation. Rodney, conversely, had conveniently reserved for himself the indulgences of still being there in Cali, of having the opportunity to say his depth and length of 'byes—and similarly, of traveling all the way down to Texas with his twelve grinning and good-times-ready groomsmen. She sensed—on a shell's slivered smile of an awareness, that she did not dare twisting, fully crack open—that Rodney and his boys would soon be careening at top speed across the states, laying their hands on whatever they could get drunk off of and smoke. And she knew too, that their eyes, dollar bills—and likely more—would be falling on whatever-the-disapproving-else she had edged out from letting her mind see, analyze, believe.

P.V. was completely within, beside herself. She had nothing to say. She turned her head up, concentrating on the window in the distance above the laptop lid, and not on the scowling image inside of it. Her partially liquefied distaste had become real chyme and had churning, frothed chunky up—creeping into her throat, mouth—its impassioned action inflaming her face. And she was struggling to swallow it, all bitter back, down. She heard Rodney blow his lips together in disgust, and mutter roughly, "*Huh*. Ok. *Later.*"

Several degrees grateful for Rodney's cue, P.V. clicked the session off without looking back at him or speaking. Rising up, she sighed, and seized a few moments to wholly breathe, from core to diaphragm to lungs all expansive and billowing out—exhaling fully out to the ready. Then pivoting—still clutching her purse in one hand—she looked down at the vacant laptop lid, and closed it with an unexpectedly forceful slap.

The restaurant was a dimly lit, self-described coffee shop in a transitional area of Fort Worth, its faded, grey stucco facade almost invisible against the dreary and ailing backdrop. Inside was bustling and aurally electric with the din of a hundred conversations, the clinking of silverware and plates, and the movement of bodies without the insulation of sound. There was a decided lack of decor in the interior, except for plastic, black picture frames containing the entity licenses legitimizing the walls, and a dull-leaved, fake floor plant that—several decades ago—someone had clearly forgotten near the cashier stand. The furniture was an inexpensive dark wood reminiscent of 1970's men's clubs and lodges, and had clearly never been replaced in the eons of the eatery's existence. But the stuffy air all around smelled comfortingly of pigs and eggs cooking, and P.V.'s rumbling, empty stomach tried to convince her eyes in 360 that that was sufficient.

Juanita bustled ahead, her slim but curvy hips swiftly navigating the twists and turns along the patron floor like a salsa dancer's at sway. Her steps were somewhat firm and powerful, but fell equally soft with a femininity, a swishing grace. She was effortlessly beautiful: a full, thick head of dark hair, parted slightly in the middle, waved out from her sculpted face like a modern-day, brown Farrah's, ensconcing a tiny, pixie-like face. Her honey-brown skin glistened almost accordingly with both the heat of the day and a quiet, inner fire. And everywhere she walked, heads turned up, scanning—male and female alike—each for their own purposes, taking in the sight of her and the cosmic, sensual pull that she emanated as she strode.

"You know, as I said, I thought you might wanna, you know, start on this end of the Dallas-Fort Worth corridor—an' then we can jus', you know, work our way back to Dallas," Juanita said, raising her voice slightly above the fray, slinking down into one of the chairs at the only empty table in the establishment. Her accent was generally clear of a Southern influence, except for a word or two here and there. Moreover, to P.V.'s discerning ears, it was clearly edged with pronunciations reminiscent of a native Spanish-speaker—and she was curious to learn exactly what type of mixture Juanita was.

Juanita took up the menu at her place setting, looking slightly about as she did so. "This place, you know—it might surprise you. But they serve some of the best, you know, *country* food in town. I know it's not, like—you know—upstyle *L.A.* or anything like *that*, but everyone knows this place, an' it's really, really *good.*" P.V. nodded at her, a tad wide-eyed. Following Juanita's lead, she sat down and took up one of the three other well-worn, plastic menus dotting the table. But she was spiritually exhausted, overwhelmed by the surreal industry of the day, and somehow, by the aging eatery of itself. And her consciousness was still on a flight, head leaning sweetly on a cool, shuttered window—bound swiftly and directly back for L.A.

"You should try the shrimp an' cheese grits," Juanita suggested, peering over a peeling edge of plastic at the top of her menu. "They're really good. An' you might wanna try the collard greens, too. Oh! An' the sweet tea—tha's like, a *must*—tha's really Texas. An' they have really good

cornbread, too...I don' know—everything's jus' really, really *good* here."
She looked up just then, in time to catch P.V.'s frowning mouth, face
angled down, eyes listlessly open but not reading. "Hey—you feeling
okay?" she asked worriedly. "I know you jus' got off the plane an'
everything—I mean, if you're not feeling well, we can always do this
another da—"

"*No*," P.V. interrupted forcefully, the thought of Rodney's sure ire at
the idea of such snapping her back into her body. "I mean, no—it's okay.
I'm like...*fine*. It's just...um..." And then she sighed, searching around for
some train of responsible thought. "...Yeah, it like, *has* been a really long
morning, but—this is really great of you, and *this*—*this* is great," she
managed, trying to muster up enthusiasm as she glanced around at the
almost depressingly dark, weltering restaurant. "So, um, no—thank you so
much. And like...*oh*—um...thank you for driving, too! And, yeah—I-I *will*
order that—um...*all* of that. It sounds great."

Juanita nodded slowly, realizing that she had seen this about twenty
times already in the few short months before—outsiders, Californians
particularly—relocating to Texas, hoping to outrun the downturning real
estate market and economy in a more cost-effective state. It had been
happening for years for other reasons, but was occurring consistently now,
and with intense urgency. And the most of them were so deer-in-
headlights-eyed yet insistent, pocketbook bottom-lines yearning for the
Southwest, but souls still clinging, sunning back, to their West Coast sands.
She sighed. They were always in a rush to find something, and to her, that
and her resultant commission were usually the only upsides of having them
flock to the state.

"Um, how old are you, P.V.—can I ask?" she ventured, observing
P.V. closely.

"Um, I'm 22? I just turned, like, a few months ago."

"Oh!" Juanita shocked, replied, smiling. "I didn' realize you were around my age."

"Wh—um, well like, how old are *you*?"

"23—I'll be 24 in December." They laughed a little together spontaneously, instantly relieved in the exhale, celebrating a same-wavelength, a generational ease with one another. Juanita gestured with her chin in the direction of P.V.'s left hand. "It's so funny—I didn' know *what* to think. I got married young, too. I mean, pretty young—for me, anyway. But...I'm not used to having California clients so young an' married! I thought that was jus'—you know—*our* thing down aroun' here, primarily."

"N—well...I mean—my parents are from Trinidad, and they married young, too, so...and, I'm really from Miami—not Cali—and there, well, a lot of people or their families are from countries that...that do that, you know, so..."

"Oh...right. Well, I mean—I get that. I'm half Mexican, so I totally understan' that part."

"You are?"

"Yeah—my Mom is from Mexico City, an' my Dad was black, from Texas. An' he grew up partly in East Texas. Tha's where they got married. So...tha's where I'm like, basically from—East Texas. A place called Beaumont." Juanita shifted uncomfortably in her chair, looking away into the crowd.

"Oh. Wow. Great mix," P.V. replied, her brain awakening in stages, already seizing in rungs up and up on gaps in what Juanita had said—and the something suddenly curious about her body language.

"Yeah, well I don' know about *that* one. If you check, the orphanages aroun' here are like, full of Mexiblack mixes like me. Seems we do a lot fun stuff together after dark, you know? But afterwards, the families—they don' all want to keep the babies, you know?"

P.V. was now fully intrigued. She promptly found herself well awake and back in her skin, oddly drawn in by what seemed to be a little mystery unfurling in front of her, from across the worn and water-stained table. She felt a bit daring, itching to ask the type of questions she was raised well not to pose. "Is that—are you—" she began. But just then, the waiter appeared—a tall, all-over dark, satin-skinned young man with big, chubby cheeks like a two-year-old's. He took their orders, bemusedly eyeing up P.V. as he did so, seemingly recording each element of her face. And then, with a sweeping flash to collect the menus, he disappeared back into the hazy, background busy, as quickly as he had come. P.V.'s foray into an inquiry seemed to have been either forgotten by Juanita amidst the bustle of the process, or she was feigning well not to have heard it, and P.V. felt instantly uncomfortable about the idea of more effectively relaunching her query.

"Anyway, you're Trini-Miami—so we like, understand each other, right?" Juanita was smiling, sitting flush back in her chair, hands crossed instinctively—carefully—atop her flat belly.

A second wave of reassurance washed over P.V., relaxing her several levels down from near anxious. "Right."

Juanita smiled again, and nodding, continued, her accent becoming more pronounced, leaning on vowels, crisping up pace. "So—i's so cool to meet a fellow realtor—I saw your pic on your brokerage page. Yours looks so much better than mine, woman. Seriously?" Then, gingerly leaning in toward P.V. and lowering her voice slightly, she added, "Actually, I totally thought I was pregnant that day. An' even though we'd been married for awhile, I wasn't ready for all that, you know? I didn' find out 'til that Friday that I wasn't. An' I swear that like, every picture I needed to take, in like, *life* I had to take that week." P.V. giggled, feeling an instant respect for Juanita's clear humility—as in actuality, she recalled that Juanita's company photo looked like the headshot of a high-end print model in a men's lifestyle magazine.

"No—*yours* is so gorgeous," P.V. protested. "But...I hear you—I couldn't even...I mean, *babies*...yeah, like, I hear you. But, yeah, I mean— they hired me when I was like, still in college. My *parents* had...*other* ideas, but I got my realtor's license at 20, so I've like, actually been working for the company for almost—almost two years now," P.V. paused, feeling a sadness come and sit suddenly on her window of freeness and light, building up big in her body. She turned her head away, toward the swirl of feeding faces, to hide her eyes, quick-welling with tears. "This wasn't my...I didn't, like, *plan* on this—to be out here and stuff...so like, I guess I'll just join whatever's—whatever brokerage is closest to what we find." She swallowed hard, turning her gaze back toward Juanita, and fully, to the business at hand. "Is yours—your brokerage—are you...are you like, happy with them?"

Juanita cocked her head to the side, eyes narrowing, examining P.V.'s face. "Yeah, pretty much, but—you know how it is right now. I mean, it's better here than for my friends an' colleagues in some other states, you know? I mean, I know you of all people know that. But that's not saying much by nothing, compared to how it *used* to be, you know? I mean, I've got inventories piling up in the system, an' it jus' wasn't like that for me a few years ago. I mean, an' like, the funny thing is, I was actually planning to leave the company altogether before all of this stuff. I mean, there's a couple a companies in town that have way less fees, an' like, better bonuses built in, better amenities—stuff like that. An' *you* know—it all adds up. Almost getting pregnant made me really think about that stuff. I mean, I was even thinking about, you know, maybe becoming a broker after that. But it's like, I can't afford to do any of that right now, you know? Like, if you're already with a company right now, an' you're just a realtor right now, I mean—it's jus' best to just stay where you are completely right now, you know?" P.V. nodded slowly, mind sorting, digesting, Juanita's absolute mouthful.

Juanita wiggled again uneasily in her chair, shaking her head and fiddling about with the plain silver place settings, dulled and stained in spots with splotches of water and time. She inclined her body further in toward P.V., voice quieter to barely audible. "Anyway," she warned, "jus' letting you know that the word on the street is to be careful about who you associate with, okay? Like every realtor an' broker is not who you need to be friends with right now, okay? I mean, we weren't hit as hard as the rest of the country with all that related mess—you know what I'm talking about. But I mean, like obviously, I'm saying we *were* hit—you know? An' that means some folks..." she sighed and shook her head, as P.V., head slightly turned to the side, uncharacteristically allowed her mouth to gape in bewildered anticipation. "...Well...it's just...my broker says she's been hearing things through the grapevine—and she believes it...she's jus' got a gut feeling about it. An' Leila—her gut, it's just like, never wrong, you know? I mean—I don't know. Jus' be careful—tha's all I'm saying. If you get a funny feeling about somebody in the industry, you should, you know—listen to it, okay?" P.V. bobbed her head in assent and sat back, wondering with a wistful ache where college had gone—to what other realm all of that fun, free, mindless time had, tongue out and taunting, skipped.

"Anyway," Juanita said dismissively, abruptly shooting up, straight-backed, to her feet. "Enough of all that. I'm gonna go wash my hands, before the waiter comes back. Two of my nurse friends have been predicting like, some kinda viral epidemic coming to Texas, so now they've got me freaking out about germs an' stuff. I don' believe it, but they say it's like, definitely gonna happen. I mean, one of them said she even had a nightmare about it, so," P.V., mouth opening wider in mini-horror, nodded her consent. And with that, Juanita turned twirl, hair flying all about her neck and shoulders. In another flash, she and her to-the-calf, high-heeled and supple, brown leather boots had already clipped halfway down the worn, tan carpet tiles toward the restroom.

The waiter passed Juanita on the way, he sailing forward, arms laden from bicep to tips with white fare-brimming bowls and steaming plates. P.V. stared well into Juanita's wake, and then turned her attention to the little bowl of collard greens being first laid down in front of her. She atypically began to eat them without waiting for her dining companion to return, the pull of their sweet scent, and the need to clear her head, calling her to them. The collards were simply beautiful in her mouth. They were a slippery, slightly unyielding, shiny, briny goodness, a pig-and-leaf flesh and flora that was magical. They were warm and wonderful, swamp things fragrant—such cuddling, lovely things, those collard greens. What Juanita had said was squarely on the money—the food simply *was* good. P.V. paused, not wanting the collards to be over so soon—in the flash of a neophyte's fork—wishing she had ordered at least two more bowls of the stuff.

"Somethin' right, honey?" the waiter asked, grinning. P.V. looked up at his chubby, milk chocolate face, which shone practically angelic against the yellow-hazed background of patron blur. He was a fist on hip, other arm still lined with plates from inner elbow to wrist, and head tilted slightly to the side—intently regarding her.

"N-no. Oh! *Ha*...yes, um..." she stammered and halted, catching his twist of phrase a few beats late. Her eyes, darting, searched his frantically for his name.

"*Tyrell*, honey," he offered breezily. "But between you an' me, e'erybody who know me call me 'Sterling'—an' for good reason, child." He smiled wider, cheeks pushing at his lower eyelids, mouth flashing teeth set in the whitest, most meticulously sculpted perfection.

"Oh! Ty…I mean—*Sterling*. Um, cool. Yeah—yes…everything's alright. Really right. I mean, like, this tastes…like…really, really lovely. I wish I had like, another bowlful and stuff. I could seriously eat this like, all day."

Tyrell beamed, upturning his big, luscious lips with pride, squinting his eyes at her with an all-too-knowing look. "Mm-*hm*! Well, Chef fled here during the hurricane 'while back. As red-haired an' green-eyed a brutha as you *e-vah* did see, honey. Freckles an' all. An' he for *sure* know what *he* doin'." And stretching out, he placed the last few dishes—piled up with steaming, ambrosial goodness—down upon the table. Unbending and pondering a second, he snappily inserted, "But as for eatin' it all day— don't you go an' do all *that* now, girl. You do, an' you jus' gon' git *fat*, honey. You got to remember this down home now—we cook wit' hog an' butter an' all kinds a thangs like that. An' jus' 'cause you don't *know* no bettah, don't mean fat gon' *be* no bettah. Hog fat ain' jus' gon' take a *holiday* on them pretty hips, y'hear?" P.V. giggled in response, and despite Tyrell's advisory, dove her fork deeply into the savory, green squish for more.

"*Girrrl*—I'm *serious*," Tyrell insisted, his face nevertheless crinkling with humor. "I *know*. Chef be hookin' some a us up *good* after hours. So now, a course, I'm fixin' to have to lose *all* this weight right *here*, honey." But as he spoke about his body, he gestured at nothing, arms fixed firmly in clenched fists on his hips. "Though honestly, girl," he continued, "the food be so good, I figure if I'm fixin' to have to *leave* this world jus' 'cause a that, then when They come git me, I'll jus' have to be like, 'mm-*hm*—I cain't argue wit' you none'—an' go on to the Nex' Realm all plump an' *peaceable*, honey." Then beaming toothily again, he winked at P.V. She laughed out loud—a short, high-pitched spurt—caught off guard by his familiarity, boyish mischievousness, and wit. Unheeding him for a second time, she dipped her fork well into, and up from, an adjacent, heaping bowlful of cheesy grits topped with lightly sautéed, jumbo shrimp.

"Mm-*hm*. I see you quiet but kinda fearless, honey. Where you from?" he inquired, cocking his head to the side again, and squinting to discern her spirit more clinically. "Ms. Juanita a friend a yours?"

"N—well...I guess so. Um, I'm a realtor too, and my husband and I need to like, find a place. And I have to start working down here, too. Um, I'm um...moving from California."

"*California? Girrrl*," Tyrell replied, grinning slyly. "I have done some *damage* up in yo' state, that's for *dang* sure. Well, there's more than a few a y'all livin' down here now—so you got comp'ny. You gon' like us here, anyway, though," then he paused, regarding her pointedly. "Now, awhile back, when you was takin' a lap in them greens, you said they was 'lovely— really, really lovely'. Now, don' take this the wrong way, honey, but—don' nobody say that about collards. I mean, they *do*—but not *that* way. So— where is you *really* from?"

"Oh! Um...Miami."

"Uh-huh...*and?*" Tyrell urged, tapping his foot—somewhat oddly, impatiently waiting.

"Well...um, my parents are from Trinidad..."

"Now *there* you go, girl! *Trinidad?* Girl, girl, *girl!* Now why didn' you jus' say somehow you had the islands in you in the *firs'* place? You see how Sterlin' be workin' *hard* up in here, so ya *know* he need to travel somewhere *sunny*, honey—an' the sooner the bettah, the way thangs goin' *these* days..." Tyrell then paused, for quite some time, staring into P.V., and then visually taking in the air all about her. His glowing, chestnut brown eyes were peculiarly scanning an invisible area near the top of her head and then up somewhere much higher, just behind her. So lengthy and strange a series of moments in silence were they, that P.V. began to feel a nearing-eerie discomfort. And she was wondering, with a climbing anxiety, what on earth—or otherwise—he was perceiving, searching for, perhaps finding.

Tyrell suddenly pulled back the intensity of his surrounding gaze, and fixing his eyes squarely on P.V.'s, said, "Well. If y'all ever...*come back* here...you know, to *visit*—even if it's a couple years from now...you an' yo'... *good husband*...don't you be no stranger, y'hear? You ask for Sterling. *I'll* still be here. 'Cause—when I'm fin'ly fixin' to...*go*...I'm 'on see the *world* then, honey—y'hear? Fixin' to see the *whole universe*...eventually. Chef keep tellin' me I need to jus'...move *on*—live my *life*, not try to be up in here *workin'* all the time. An' he right 'bout that, girl—he right. I know he is. But...I don' know what it is—I jus' *worr'* 'bout the place all the time...An' I tell you what *else*—there's somethin' that-that *happened* 'roun' here—up the road a piece...somethin' that I jus'...I jus' cain't git *past*. An' I need to take care a that, honey—cain't have that on my *mind* when I'm *travelin'*. Now, I ain' ready *now*, but—you check in on ol' Sterlin' like I told you, even if it's a couple years, y'hear? I'm 'on want some...*thangs* from you before I go—travel tips, an' *blessin's* an' whatnot—an' you gon' be...*y'all* gon' be jus' the folk to help me—y'hear me Miss Trinidad? Y'hear? Okay?"

"O...*kay*..." P.V., profoundly bewildered, hesitantly replied. The hairs on the back of her neck, as if on cue, stood on end and remained—like sticks up straight—there, and she suddenly, involuntarily, shuddered. She looked down instinctively at her left arm. It was covered with seemingly infinite rows of tiny, but pronounced, goose pimples. She slid her right hand up and down it, to quell the orderly, little puckers of fear, and attempted to switch thoughts in order to calm herself. But a thick, viscous, grey of unknown and illogic was swirling in, overpowering, her mind as regards Tyrell's odd, lengthy stare, the meaning and weight of his words, and the rippling fright she had just experienced.

Tyrell suddenly smiled, deliberately and slowly, a foot perched just behind him, body poised to back himself away from the table. He seemed to have fully regained his breezy composure. "Now you jus' remember what I *said*, honey," he half-teased again. "Don't you go fallin' in love wit' them greens jus' ta be reckless now—'cause you gon' *wanna*—an' that an' e'erythang else you eat down here jus' gon' put some serious pounds on them hips. An' trust me—you don't wanna go down *that* road. Ain't good for the *belt* nor the *health*, honey—you listen to ol' Sterlin' now, y'hear? But…I see how you are, so…if you don' listen, jus' remember to go git yo'se'f a personal trainer, if you wanna keep lookin' an' breathin' like you is. An' thankfully, we got more than enough a *them* runnin' aroun' down here, to accommodate folks when they ain't *tryin'* to be *wise*."

P.V. began to have a feeling. It was a traveling, inching awareness of Tyrell's spirit. And it was creeping up, up into her head, mind—a message for her in its mouth—from the thick, outer rind of her soul. But, just before she was able to discern its content, she heard herself say, "Well, like…um, yeah—sure. I'll like, definitely do that. I, um…I wasn't sure I'd like it here, but…um, you know—maybe…maybe I will."

"Well," Tyrell said flatly, knitting his brow, then whole countenance smoothing out into a glistening, sweet cocoa emotionlessness. He was a study no longer in the seeming ribbing or the cautionary, but in the still, outer quality of fine stone. He wafted a hand out, firmly rearranging the order of some of the bowls and plates directly in front of P.V. Then he looked up, and half-pivoted slowly, casting her a mysterious, all-cells-penetrating side glance. "I tell you *what*, honey. It's jus' like what they say 'bout the North Texas weather—'if you 'on't like it, well, jus'…*stick aroun'* awhile.'" And in an instant—carrying only a circular, spotless black serving tray from nowhere in his long, elegant hands—he smiled slightly at her from one corner of his mouth, and bowed reverently. Then snapping his head and x-ray eyes away, he slid—a little *too* quickly—back into the people.

"Girl—*hardwood floors*?" Rodney remarked, toeing a section of the gleaming—seemingly wormholed—dark-stained slats in the foyer cautiously. He jerked his head up, as if awakening, and breezed a kiss to P.V.'s cheek as he and his mammoth, rolling designer suitcase fully entered the unit. His breath smelled of grain alcohol and spearmint, but his lips were cool and comforting to the skin. He was swathed in the hearkening, musky wondrousness of his fave cologne, and it made P.V. realize that despite all of the shenanigans, she had somehow missed him. Thankfully too, he had arrived without his twelve groomsmen, who, after assisting him in dropping off both of their vehicles, were no doubt already en route to start—or continue another—night of unconscionable skylarking.

"*Faux. Faux* hardwood floors. Like, you know—wood laminate," P.V. explained nervously, hand leaving the nickel doorknob, following in his wake.

"And a muh fuckin' museum-piece chandelier, I see," Rodney observed, eyeing up the gleaming, 9-light, brushed nickel chandelier, waving its contemporary, glass-shaded tiers out almost exactly like the branches of a Christmas tree. Magnificent and sculptural, it was one of the most prominent features in the tastefully decorated formal living room in front of them. P.V. took a closer look at Rodney's profile, as head cocked to the side, and seemingly almost transfixed, his gaze traversed the hallelujah arms of the chandelier, and the complementing, pastel grey ceiling and walls. He had cleared his face entirely of the thick, professorial beard that he had let hedge there over the weeks, and now appeared nearer to her age again. But his mood was still a mix of the strained personhood that had popped up ever since he had made the decision for them to move, and the too-cool teenager who had casually eased his way first into her giggles, and then into her womanhood. And she realized that she somehow desperately wanted, needed the latter back—and not that school-dad version of Rodney, who had caused them to uproot from the place of good friends and big water, to whatever the *this* was that she had been forced to arrange, oversee.

"Y—well, I mean...but it was like, *totally* cheap for them, Roddie— remember? Like, um, remember when I e-mailed you all the paperwork? And texted you? Like, I mean, I *told* you the owners had put a little money into renovating the place, but like, not that much—that like, the guy grew up with like, a builder for a father, and so they just like, did it themselves, because they like *doing* that kinda stuff. And I mean, like, they *installed* stuff like that just to make it *look* cool, to make it *look* like, kind of expensive— but like, on a *total* budget, Roddie. Remember? I mean, they're like, *our* age and like, *normal* about that stuff, Roddie..." She halted, her mind reeling back to when she and Juanita were zipping along the looping DFW highways, in Juanita's impressively massive, black luxe and shiny, U.S.- make pickup truck. They had initially paused here and there at reasonably- priced residential listings in Arlington and Fort Worth. There was so much buzzing about the easy, walking city that was Fort Worth's downtown, but the screeching, swooping flocks of small brown birds—swarming and settling upon high-wires, buildings, street signs—ultimately held P.V. back. "Grackles," Juanita explained. "Like clockwork, you know? Every time, 'round this time of year." Something about them had nevertheless intrigued rather than repelled P.V. She found their squawking, whistling, dark communities compelling—just a part of the default oddities in this new, sun-blanched and stretching state. But she could already see Rodney, who typically ran mildly indifferent to edging on hostile in the presence of animals—a feeling mutually shared by any animal in his vicinity—texting her a bitch about them everyday until they could square the dimes to move again. So, at her urging, Juanita pressed on, pedal to the floor on the interstate, back through to Arlington.

Residential Arlington seemed largely an evenly-planned series of tract home communities-upon elaborate custom tracts; endless sudden clearings revealing clean, stark churches of almost every denomination; painstakingly planted young trees; and island after island of strip malls—after row after row of chain restaurants. On either side of the highway, they also passed its bustling theme-parks—but she knew the Vegas-jaunting Rodney could not live there and consider himself still breathing: he would be forever absent to the condensed haunts of their last stop—Dallas. And too, after all of her subsequent sojourns with Juanita that day—in and amongst its varied corridors—P.V.'s spirit itself wanted to live amongst Dallas' creeks, lakes, river. She missed, was in need of, the curling up and spraying Pacific ocean—open expanse and endless—but, much smaller bodies, beckoning and soul-soothing, would do. So, she chose a great space on the outskirts of the glinting glass of Uptown Dallas, well tucked in and amongst the residential activity of the people—for Rodney, because of its proximity to the stadium where his fave, pro basketball, was played. But subsequently, as she inked the deal for their new place in the "D" as Juanita called it, her mind suddenly flipped scenes of the condo search, in quick-time—resting curiously, uneasily, on a statue she had seen outside a strip shopping mall, near the suburbs of Fort Worth. The outdoor sculpture was of a man in a nicely-fitted suit, bowing low—the crown of his hat squarely cupped in the palm of his outstretched hand.

"Yeah, but dis kinda *nice*," Rodney insisted, strolling the perimeter of the unit, tapping at walls. "I mean, it's a one-bedroom—wit' a den—right? An' we clearly used ta way more dan *dat*. I mean—it's no *house* an' shit. An' a course, we used ta, you know, *huh*—*way* heavier furniture an' shit. But— dis still kinda *nice*. I mean, it's kinda *chic* an' shit—considerin' dat dey really

countryfolk, an' whatnot. An' I mean *still*—even if it was all *nekked* an' shit—
dis place would *still* be lookin' kinda good as a muh. I 'ont' know—got
some good *bones* an' design about it, a *somethin'*. So, seriously den, Wifey—
what's da catch?" He was steeped in being wholly unconvinced that there
wasn't a scam afoot—constructed by his pretty-faced, realtor wife. And as
he paused deeper into the floor plan, surveying the crisp, pastel tan dining
room walls—with their elegant, contemporary nickel light switch plates and
ringing, triple-ridged crown moulding—his mind kept trying to discern
where the secret money trap was hidden.

"Well, um, Roddie—remember like, that I told you that like, because
of the market, they kind of basically can't afford to get rid of this right
now? I mean, it's like, the last few good deals went for their *neighbors'*
places, without a hitch, but when *they* tried to sell *this* place, they just
weren't getting offered like, what they needed from it. And their whole
thing was like, you know—fix it up cheap and then get a good deal on it, so
they could afford something like, way bigger. I mean, like, with a backyard
and a pool and stuff. I mean, Roddie—they've already got a kid, and the
wife, she's like, *pregnant*—remember? So they're like, kind of like, really
desperate for more space right now. Remember—her parents have a ranch
like, way out somewhere in a place called Weatherford? So they like,
decided to just move back in with them, and make a little money or at least
break even or something renting this place out—I mean, 'til the market
picks back up? I mean, including the furniture in the deal—letting us use
it—it just like, saves them on storage fees and stuff. That's all." P.V. took
a breath, feeling a wave of irritation undulate within, up through her. She
was exhausted of the trying to please Rodney in a decision that had not
been hers from the outset. And reminding him of conversations regarding
it, that had already been spoken to him and to the air, simply intensified her
feelings of helplessness and frustration. Her memories of the warm, savory
collard greens, and oddly beckoning shock at the sight of the shrewd-eyed

and screeching, little brown birds, were fading. And she felt, saw, herself again, cheek resting as she snoozed on the cool pane of a window—as its surrounding, big, metal bird touched down in L.A.

"Uh-*huh*," Rodney muttered. "I mean, I know people hurtin' all over an' whatnot…*huh*—we still cain't even afford to sell *our* ol' place for shit, either. But—even wit' all *dat*, dey lease on dis for us *still* seem way cheaper dan it should be."

"Yeah, but like, *Roddie*…I mean—you were…right about Texas…I mean, in that—they don't tend to ask as much for leases as they would in Cali. I mean, like, the dollar *does* go way farther here, even when you're talking about real estate. But…like I said, this was so way discounted because of the way the market's gone, too. I mean, it's not as bad here with all of that, but like…I mean, like, they're still *feeling* it. So the owners *had* to have it fixed up like, really nice if they wanted to like, *sell* it in this kind of market. I mean, like—this is an older building too, so keep that in mind. And I mean, Roddie—we could totally buy this place from them whenever we're ready again, and like, fix it up the way we want. I mean, they're really, really up for…open to that. I mean, us buying it and stuff." Rodney nodded, processing her hesitating, pleading chatter—noting that she sounded somewhat like a child who was worriedly trying to ease her parent into keeping a stray dog. And at his core, he enjoyed that feeling of her anxiousness around him. And then he walked back past a doorless room they had initially passed—and finally looked into it.

"Oh, *uh-uh! Jackpot*—an', what da *fuck*, Wifey? It's like da mutha fuckin' *country club mess* up in here! *Daaaamn*! Lookin' like you gon' have ta wear pearls an' heels an' shit in here when you gittin' yo' cook on. Uh-*huh*. Got *yo'self* a *fly*-ass kitchen, sexy! *Huh*. All dis fat-ass granite an' tile—"

"*Faux* granite—it's like, a man-made production," P.V. interrupted nervously. "And—and the floors are like, hand-painted to *look* like good tile." Rodney nevertheless went like biblical Thomas to the counter tops, probing and scratching at them, searching for—and finding—tell-tale off-textures and seams. Then he comically bent his extra-long body down from the waist to the floor in a fold, like a yogi, head turned completely to one side and just inches from the ground. Lips upturned in an exaggerated pout, he played at eyeing up the effortlessly coordinating, tony-looking tile.

"Uh-*huh*. Okay. Lettin' you off da hook dere, Wifey. *Daaang. Huh*—dey nicknames *mus'* be 'Faux1' an' 'Faux 2' for real though, huh? *Hahahahaha*! It's like da two a dem da king an' queen a mutha fuckin' plastic an' shit. *Wow.*" He was grinning, relaxing, hands on hips and tapping at the tile with the toe of one of his swag, black suede leather workman's boots. P.V. giggled—for the first time in weeks—sighing on the tail of all of those high-pitched bubbles, in a relief that Rodney seemed back to his old, fun self again. And she told herself that because of such, everything would be okay: it would be just like Cali again—like roomies with benefits again—if that was truly what marriage was.

"I 'on't know, Wifey—you sure dey names really Trudy an' Nick, an' not mutha fuckin' Barbara an' Kenneth from da land a mutha fuckin' make-believe, by-way-a-Malibu an' shit? I mean, is dey both blonde? Do dey have a dream house an' a muh fuckin' plastic-ass townhome? Do dey arms unbend? Do da chick be walkin' all up on her tippy-toes like she walkin' on huge-ass gaps an' shit? *Hahahahaha—yo*—you gotta take note a dese things when you be doin' dese out-a-town deals an' shit, Wifey! *Hahahahaha*—whooo! Oh, well. It's cool, Wifey—I ain't a hater. I ain't mad at 'em. *Now* I see da mutha fuckin' *discount, hahahahaha*–whooo! Guess all dey toy-works is helpin' *us* work a muh fuckin' miracle an' shit, huh? *Hahahahahahaha—faux-ass* couple. I *luh* dem two! *Shiiit*—lettin' us do da Big D kinda right, huh? *Hahahahahahaha*—ohhh! *Huh.* Now jus' imagine if all dis shit was real. I mean, *daaamn*—what *is* real up in dis mutha fucka, Wifey?"

For two weeks, Rodney was wholly himself—amusingly, charmingly, human. "*Daaaamn*, girl," he cracked appreciatively, sliding into the kitchen behind P.V. in his sock-clad feet, kissing her cheek, embracing her from behind. She had just arrived back from a long day of employee orientation at the local branch of her realty company, and subsequently driving around the breadth of Dallas with her new broker. Yet already, domestically industrious that she had become, she had the cool gases of air in the little, rented condo swimming hot and delicious with the enticing minglings of fresh, simmering beef; cinnamon; curry spices; and a strong back-of-the-throat kick from some wildly tossed in habañero pepper.

Rodney positioned his face to view straight down P.V.'s chest, enjoying that the fleshy tops of her ample, tan breasts were peeking above the tank top she had tucked inside her suit coat. "Uh-*huh*—I see my *friends* out ta-*day*! Uh-*huh*," he joked, and, pouting his lips, he pulled the front lapels of her jacket together, in a feigned attempt to conceal her chest entirely. "*Girrrl*—you got ta put all dat *away*! I 'on't want no otha men's *eyes* all up in yo' scrumptious *ladies*!" P.V. giggled in reply, angling a pot lid halfway on an apparatus of goodness heating up on one of the blue-flame burners.

"Mm-*hmm*," he teased. "You laughin'. You need what my uncle said my gra'ma-ma used ta call 'foundation garments.' Jus' *look* at all *dis*—all yo' *scrumptious lusciousness* jus' a spillin' all out like pig grease an' shit, girl. *Mm*!" P.V. giggled forth anothre sweet, bubbling stream of mirth in response. She was delighted that Rodney's comedic side had somehow resurfaced, despite the persistent march of incredibly strained days.

"Ahhh, *yes*. Mm-*hmm*," Rodney continued, raising an index finger in mock self-righteous speech, cheeks puffing at trying not to laugh. "You know, a propah lady's figure *begin* wit' a good *foundation*, Wifey." Then closing his eyes, he turned his face—well above her head—away, in a pretense of disapproval, shielding himself from his view of her bosom. "So, ma'am, given dat you ain't wearin' what I'm gon' call da propah *foundational garments*, I'm a have ta ask you nicely *ag'in* ta put all yo' *delicious, round, fine*—*ooh* dey *is* fine, ain't dey—jus' a luscious, quick-risin' muffinfolk *away*!" They both descended into laughter at his routine, bodies melting and folding into each other. Rodney could usually withhold his own as he joked, but the days without work were transforming him into less the controller, more the vulnerable, even unto himself.

"*Ayyy* though—seriously, it smell damn *good* up in here, Wifey. An' spicy-*hot*, yo! What you cookin' up, girl—you sure we still in America? You takin' a bruh' tummy on a lil' island vacay? An'—what's *that*?" Rodney asked, glancing at the conical, terra cotta-colored contraption on the black and steel, gas-burning stove.

"Oh, um—a tagine." P.V. replied, raising her eyebrows and looking up at him expectantly, tacitly encouraging him to guess at the cuisine for that evening's meal.

He thought for a moment, playfully upturning his lips again. Then he cocked his head to the side, peering at her out of the corner of his eyes. "Morocco?" he offered, drawing a look of drop-jaw shock from her.

"*Ha*—yah!" she responded enthusiastically, laughing and shrugging in surprise at his recognition. "Um, like, totally! Actually trying to do a quickie, like, Texan version…um…beef instead of lamb, browning it first, using local peppers—stuff like that. Mummy picked up this cool, like, easy tagine pot on holiday in London, so I'm like, trying it out."

Rodney nodded approvingly. "Mm-*hm*! Well den, a brutha bettah wash up—an' git his Texas *belly dance* on," he announced, grinning. Releasing his hug, he began to sway, jiggling his head and torso from side to side. His arms were out in a wingspan, jerking too energetically towards his shoulders, long fingers rhythmically snapping. And in tandem, he was humming a hilariously childish sounding, makeshift tune, to accompany his movements. P.V. erupted into giggles again, holding onto the counter for support, temporarily unable to continue working through his sweet and endearing silliness.

But the days and nights crawled painfully on afterwards, and it was clear that the whosoevers Rodney had said he knew in Texas were not willing—or able—to help him find a job. He immediately began responding to the few applicable want-ads that spoke to his expertise, promptly reporting to the handful of interviews that he secured from them. Dutifully too, he descended upon every networking event in the city and surrounding areas, in the multitudinous hours of space in between. But always, he returned to the little, rented condo unit at nights a well-dressed, frustrated—and empty-handed—young man. Temporary agencies, his last resort, were even less assistive—he applied and interviewed at a few, but they always advised him that they were already having difficulty securing openings in general, and that in his field in particular, practically no one was hiring. And it all showed upon him. He was less of a leaning flex in the body as the weeks rolled quickly forward, and more the unshiny lanky—his lean, athletic form turning into a stretch of scrawn, like a gawky, beanstalk of a teenager whose flesh had not yet caught up to his hastily spiraling-up frame.

P.V. conversely, had previously gotten herself together and voted in the historic presidential election, and lovingly began a household campaign of making Rodney's fave junk meals—with a grown-up twist—to cheer him up and show her support for him. Her tiny kitchen put forth hearty, big-girl-and-boy homemade pot pies; and endless higher-brow, but well-budgeted, variations of macaroni and cheese—all paired with inexpensive local wines and beers. But it still rained heavily, swift slant and grey, both outside and inside their long, leased windows. She was hustling for buyers and sellers, and ferrying what seemed like ceaseless smatterings of picky and particular clients around town—only to meet Rodney's dark cloud again, as persistently non-generating, he moodily slipped a fork into yet another of her consolation creations.

"I networked my *ass* off today, Wifey," he would say in between slow, despondent chews. "*Nuthin.* And dat other job I applied to? *Nuthin.* Dey ain' never even call me *back.* Shit. You lucky, wit' yo' real estate career an' shit—even if y'all cain't make' it rain nowadays. *Huh.* Try runnin' yo' ass all over da towns, jus' steady lookin' for a damn job." And that was the being married to him, night after night. And over each plate, bowl, glass, stein, it became clearer to P.V. that restarting a home together during strange times, in a strange territory—surrounded by other people's furniture—had truly faulted the foundation of their little union. And somewhere too, she painfully again, and in deeper degrees, realized that that very couples' bond of itself they seemed to have once had was actually haphazardly mixed from a nothingness—that they knew nothing pivotal of the underperson of each other, that they had slapped their lives together with naught stronger or more adhesive than children's play putty and washable safety glue.

But, in the very late evenings, something even more troubling began. Rodney arrived back at the condo later and later in the nights—missing P.V.'s meals entirely—and always with eyes red and bloodshot, breath reeking to all perimeters around him of seemingly endless hard rounds of alcohol. And no sooner did his foot hit the threshold, than he would locate P.V. and shove himself—heavy and weaving—upon her, demanding sex like an insistent bull, pushing her little frame back toward the bedroom. He would thrust himself upon and into her all night, over and over and over again—long body blanking out her struggling away, senses ignoring or oblivious to her protestations, screams, visible pain. And so, all of an instance, in the accruing of days, there was no more laughter in their household—and there were no more rights, except for Rodney's own. And for P.V., there was also no 'no'.

P.V. telephoned her mother, deliberately not telling her of the terrors being wrought against her body in the nights, not relaying that which was happening to her very own selfhood. She concentrated only on the latest as regarded her and Rodney's finances in the new territory—which included the continuing saga that was his career downfall.

"*P.V.*," lilting, and casual for the moment in tongue, her mother was beginning to strenuously speak a wisdom above her own din of opening and closing pots, stirring and shaking off spoons at the edge of cast iron pans, and tending the constant bubbling of savories in liquid. "Men does *smell* you, yuh know. Deh does tek yuh scent like somet'ing *hunted*, an' promptly *learn up all* yuh *weaknesses*. An' mind you—men does tek *full advantage* a yuh weaknesses, when deh does feel de *need*. Oh, yes! An' I *tol'* you already yuh Faddah an' I could *tell* dat one yuh married was not for *you*—maybe one a he groomsman-friends at de weddin'—but *not dat one*."

"Mum!" P.V. objected softly, nervously doodling on the skin at the top of her left hand as she did so. She was absentmindedly inscribing herself with dark blue ink, in a jagged pattern of v's—like a row of shark's teeth—across and sloping down from the pinky.

"'Mum' *nuttin'*! I didn' *want* dis fuh yuh, P.V.! But you too *quick*—marry up deh *firs' mahn* who yuh body *t'ink* it *want* in dat Freeness Place yuh lef' yuh *good home* wit' yuh Faddah an' me for—t'inking you know it *ahl, ahl, ahl*. You t'ink 'cause I ole I *dotish*? I know e-v'ry*t'ing* dat happened to mek you *t'ink* you should marry dat mahn."

P.V. stayed silent, heart pounding. If her mother could suss out that Rodney had been her first and only lover, then P.V.'s new, darker secret was not safe either. And it was an agony that she was too ashamed to tell, have revealed—a rabid thing gnawing at her that she hoped would turn a spooky tail and scurry away. If she told her mother, then those decades-old pots with all their baked-in love and flavors—transported from Trinidad to Toronto to London to Miami—would go flying, accompanied by the dissonance of a loud shriek followed by pitch-high, incessant wailing. And her mother *would* go so far as to bend forward retching, spitting up food, chunks of chyme, and even bile, telling her in between labored breaths how she had never heard of such unspeakable, unspeakable, unspeakable things before—and never wished to again. And then there her matriarch would be, without P.V. to assist her—on the floor in the high suburbs of Miami in an enveloping shock, grasping at her heart and housedress in a state of being overcome, crying out for her husband and her live-in housekeeper to come and help her. Thereafter too, would be the heartbreaking silences, the icy-hot emotional distancing—and in her mother's eyes, whenever they visited with each other, a reified and quick-maturing, head-dropping shame.

"P.V., lemme tell you some*t'in'*—you t'ink *bed* does mek you a 'oman? You t'ink on top it ahl—jus' like dat—*married* does mek you a 'oman? Well. Is now you see what 'omanhood is truly ahl about—if yuh marry wrong, it mean deh *t'in* an' not de *t'ick*, eh? Yuh see it now? Ah? Jus' *look* at what you let dat mahn sink you into—jus' *look* at it!" Her mother kissed her teeth in true West Indian fashion, a scowling sound that screeched and sucked disapprovingly from the inside of gums across bone. "You know my marriage to yuh Faddah was arranged. An' *you* know I could 'ave done dat wit' *you*, but I said, 'no—she born in de *West*, le' she mek she own decisions.' But, yuh Faddah t'ought differently—an' you know he gon' say dis is ahl *my* fault—you know is *he* who did still wahnt to marry you off. If I had *listened* to m'husban', indeed you could a marry *well*—decent family, *ex-*

ce-llent providah, wealth for yuh *days*. Yuh hear me? Wealth for yuh *life*, P.V.!
But you young people ahl tek up wit' dis *sex* t'ing—*sex an' sex an' sex an' sex*.
Who wahnt who, an' wha' yuh *wahnt* an' wha' yuh *don' wahnt*…well. Yuh
see, *my* Muddah—yuh *Nani*—she did always seh, 'girls always so *troublesome*,
honey—*always*!' An' here, see nuh—I *live* to see is *true*."

"*Mum*!" P.V. pleaded, hurting worse to her spirit's core. She put
down the pen, having scrawled over the entirety of her left hand. Rising
and wincing, she limped to her rented kitchen, to occupy her hands with
industry and minimize the inadvertent parental stabbing at her secret
emotional wounds.

"Well?" her mother replied casually, clanking a pot lid firmly down.
"P.V.—lemme tell yuh some*t'in'*—dat young man can't love you! I can see
it in he *face*. Somet'ing happened to him—I don't know *what*—an' he can't
love. Not *yet*. He need ahl kinda *healin'*, P.V.! An' he gon' *hurt* you
m'daughtah—he gon' hurt you *badly*. *Listen* to yuh Muddah. Fuh *once*—*listen*
to me, nuh. An' when he hurt you *once*, he gon' hurt you *again*, P.V.! Dog
mus' return to he bone—'til he *bury* it, or it *finish*."

P.V. had opened the fridge, shakily beginning her night's prep of a
dinner for one, but her mother's words were piercing and haunting and
everywhere. They were in the crisp air of the tall but skinny, gleaming,
stainless steel fridge; in the sapphire and motley-other-blue gas flames
flickering, licking up from a burner at an old pot on the stove; in the most
oxidized of the worn places on the metal pot spoons lying in wait on the
side counter; and in the funky cuts of just-butchered raw beef rolling
bloody pink water down white paper. And they were rolling around and
around inside her head like too many marbles, bouncing and popping at
things and pins and hurting them. And she had nothing to say to the
wisdom, and it had everything to say to her.

And so it continued between P.V. and Rodney—without report to others or reprieve. He was repeatedly pushing in on all of her boundaries, either deliberately or recklessly—the next day, always using his joblessness and drunkenness as his excuse for being so relentless on and in her body. Without a way out, P.V. began to secrete her selfhood down and inward, like a turtle being attacked on all sides: she became a presence without words, a person without agency or opinion. But then one day without warning, Rodney thankfully—but mysteriously—stopped coming home most nights, at all.

The month of All Souls had long since descended, its weeks turning onto the street of Peace and Gratitude's pre-holiday, and P.V. felt isolated. She felt trapped by the misery of Rodney and the things he painfully, repeatedly wrought upon her flesh—the things that he made her do and have done to her in that rented bedroom—on the nights when he even bothered to return home. And in the air, too, whether he was absent or present was the reality of his joblessness, decreasing ambition, and otherwise complete spiral downward. She made a cup of tea—a strong brew Earl Grey by infusion, of leaves sent to her by her mother as a mini-housewarming gift. Walking gingerly across the floor, twinges of pain shocking out from between her thighs, she stood at the window, numbly looking down across the parking lot—and began to analyze herself. Adulthood had clearly onset lightning fast and hideous, and everything was too real—so quickly—and not retarding. She realized too, that whilst she had not been certain before what to call herself, that one in the bathroom mirror every morning was something more of a woman now, because of everything dark that was happening, and how belly up and floating things had become. Marriage *was* making her into a woman—and a decidedly ripped and worn one, at that.

P.V. reasoned in her head that she could let Rodney continue to set the new pace—a grey cloud over both of them, no way out of the in—or she could try to carve out a life for herself in the light. And with that, she reminded herself that back in Cali, when the bottom began to fall out of their sweet life, at least they had a cadre of good friends to run with, commiserate with—along bonds that were fixed, that did not change. They had the familiarity of surroundings there, places they knew, places in which they had invested a history. Those spaces for them in time had been inadvertently shaped in large part, by the friendships they had formed as individuals, long before they had met or married each other. So, in the spirit of retrieving the all of that back, she decided to share her tea—to pick up her smartphone and answer Juanita's seemingly million voice messages and texts. And that led to her cooking lunch for Juanita and her stay-at-home-mom-friend Georgina, that very afternoon.

P.V. held the dark grey condo unit door open for them, noting fully into herself how dull, forlorn, and uniform it was—just like the ones almost perpendicularly to the left and right of it. For the first time in awhile, she felt the tug of missing her and Rodney's revamped, and uniquely itself, California home. She drew a deliberate uptake of the perfume of the two new people, in an attempt to distract herself from feeling the old, shut away and swirling emotions—from remembering all of the heart-tugging, sunny good times behind her.

Where Juanita was built almost like a living Barbie doll—tall, lithe, slightly curvy about the bust and hips—Georgina was closer in height to the petite P.V., and leaning on the fine-boned, without seemingly an ounce of flesh. The young mother was extraordinarily constructed like a track athlete—one of the more squat, sinewy-muscled ones—and she wore her dark hair cropped neatly all about her deep brown face.

"*Girrrl*, I *like* y'alls condo!" Georgina gushed, patting at the plush, cream-colored, modular sofa, and eyeing up its neatly coordinating, dalmatian-pattern-on-cream side chair, with its dark, faux wood feet. "Reminds me a times when I was in school, girl! Had got myself this *cute* lil' apartment—an' had a roommate who was goin' to my school an' everythang. *Shoooooot*—an' you couldn' tell the two of us *nuthin*! We thought we was *livin'*, honey!"

"I wish we had more room," P.V. replied distantly. Her inner thoughts were simply unable to be stifled. They were walking her back in a wistful 360 through her and Rodney's California house, as if at a realtor's open—room to room, thing upon thing, space upon space. It had been an ample home for a new couple—a yellow sun, warm and shining all around them. For such awhile too, it had been a place of easy being and breathing. It was their ship, their vessel together. And every bruise-filled night and new-scarred day, she was beyond wishing they had stayed there and waited out the economic storm until the waters subsided. For, they had both needed to grow more, be honed more—especially Rodney.

"*Girrrl*, y'all need to move farther out when y'all get ready—an' when it's time again. That's what Deacon an' I was goin' to do, before the market got funny," Georgina remarked.

"Yeah," P.V. responded, sighing and sinking down onto the low-bearing, Dalmatian-patterned ottoman at the feet of the corresponding side chair. "That would be...*yeah*...Um, where do you both live?"

"*Ooooooh*—South Dallas, girl. Ha-*ha*! You'll learn," Georgina replied, chuckling, exchanging glances with Juanita.

"An' Beau an' I are in East Dallas. You have to come visit us sometime soon, chica." Juanita added. P.V. nodded, recalling the drive around Dallas with her broker-boss on her first day of work. In her mind, she remembered an intriguing, art-deco-esque office building that rose brick red and clean, high above the rooftops of South Dallas. She was next driven, hustling along, down some of its stark back streets. But, she hadn't really seen enough of it to gauge fully what Georgina meant. And equally, the broker had steered them almost impatiently through East Dallas, only pausing to point out Swiss Avenue, with its row after row of stately, squarely-built historic homes. Many of those manors already lay spiked from their well-manicured lawns, with various and sundry 'For Sale' and 'For Rent' signs.

"Well, *dang*, girl—you didn' have to do all that! We didn' come here to have you slave all mornin'!" Georgina blurted out, eyes catching the heaping plates of golden brown Trinidadian patties, samosas, and rolled roti and curry. They were perfect and inviting, surrounded thoughtfully by their corresponding accompaniments of various, brightly-hued chutneys, jellies, and pickled vegetables.

"Oh! Um…it's my pleasure. My Mum and my Nan—my *Grandmum*--taught me how to cook…well, Trinidadian food anyway…and like, we just don't know the meaning of like, *enough* and stuff. So please, please, please, um…help yourself," P.V. replied shyly, dutifully waiting for the women to sit down.

"Well, *girrrl*—if I pig out, don't be mad *at* me! Them kids a mine git all the food first—that's my rule. *Ooh*—before I forget, this Deacon here," Georgina said, extending her flip cell phone to P.V., having pulled up his photo on its tiny screen. He was a jet black-skinned man—smooth, ebony, and effortless—and somewhat chubby in the face. His eyes and expression were so soft and endearing, that P.V. stared curiously at the picture for quite some time. In the photo, he was sporting a tan, fedora-like hat, and underneath a white chef's apron peeked out a matching tan suit, and corresponding grey and tan tie. There was a line of sweat running along one side of his face, and beads of perspiration about the visible portion of his forehead. He looked like what he was—a sweet-spirited husband and father, industriously grilling up somethings for his beloveds. The picture was of a moment—a clearly snapped sliver of time when he wasn't ready—as it was blurred about the hands, and his mouth was slightly open but smiling, as if pleasantly surprised. That was what stirred P.V. the deepest. The photographer had captured the very goodness, light, and love in his soul, had fresh caught what was actually there.

Conversely, her photos of Rodney were not like that—they never were. On film, he was always smirking, or one eyebrow up, or simply grinning mischievously. There was always an underlying hardness to his image, and an unseemly one-upsmanship—as if he knew more than the viewer, and was in on a bigger, grander joke and scheme than the same.

"He's so sweet-faced," P.V. finally remarked softly. "Um, what does he do—um, work? Where does he work?"

Georgina grinned with pride, pursing her lips together. "*Hmm*. I know—ain't he? New car salesman out there at one a them big mega parks—I'll show you. Been takin' care a me an' all our kids wit' dat. Girrl, I *know* I've been blessed—jus' a *good*-hearted man! E'eryday wit' him is what he is—a blessin', girl! Oh—I took that picture by the way."

"Fourth of July?" P.V. inquired.

"Ooh, girl, *no*! That day, I'd a wished it was—that woulda made some sense! *Hahaha*! *Girrrl*, no—it was a Sunday mornin', right before we was all fixin' to leave for church—an' that's a caravan an' a *production*, lemme tell you. It take two suv's an' a whole mess a toys an' juice boxes just to *git* us there all at the same time. Anyway, here I realized this man *outside*, child—what else, *grillin*'. An' gettin' himself good an' smellin' like hog an' smoke—right before services—in the process! So, I snuck my little self right up on him. He didn' hear nothin' 'cept all that sizzlin' an' combustion noise he was makin'. I snuck right up on him, an' I says, 'Mister—*what* is you doin'?'

An' he looked up, almost jumped clear out his skin, an' then right after that, we jus' steady started laughin'. An' then he come says to me, 'uh, now, I was jus' whippin' up some good eats, Ma'am—for you an' some a the little ones for later.' Girrrl. Jus' a good-hearted *man*!" She sat back and smiled contentedly, fingers absent-mindedly flipping through the rest of her phone gallery for P.V.

"He *is* jus' a really nice man," Juanita agreed, nodding in Georgina's direction. "We're always grilling at the house, an' he an' Gina come over—with great stuff, too—an' we all jus' like, talk an' hang out for hours. He an' Beau have like, barbecue competitions an' stuff. They're hilarious."

Georgina chortled, eyes upturned to the heavens, shaking her head. "They is *sooo* ridiculous wit' all that 'which-state-barbecue-the-best' mess. *Hahahahaha*! An' then, they be eatin' up e'ery last piece of flesh on they plates—of the other person's barbecue—an' steady laughin' an' still talkin' 'bout how they state is the best. *Mens*. See how they are?"

"Right?" Juanita concurred, head back and laughing. "Like there any leftovers after that. It's like—what's that cartoon? Like Fred an' Barney, you know?"

P.V. smiled weakly at it all, a jealous twinge snapping in the middle of her chest like a bully at a rubber band, over their easy camaraderie, and breezy, loving, married lives. They were not just *with* their spouses, they were clearly loved by them and *friends* with them. And they were friends with each other. And everything just seemed to work so well for all of them, the four together—so aggravatingly well.

"How, um—how did you meet Deacon?" P.V. asked, pouring herself a large, wishfully anesthetizing glassful of her homemade, blood-red sangria.

"How did we—oh, *girrr*! *Hahahahaha*—now *that's* a *story*! Juanita know it already. Okay—catch this—I be such a *mess* sometimes, girl. I met D at that same café in Fo' Wor' where you an' Nita had lunch the other day. You know, *e'erybody* go dere—*sometime* or the other. Heck, I was jus' hangin' out—nineteen—visitin' my cousin who used to work there then. Girl—*T*—he was so nice! Jus' like a brother to me. An his lil' face was so cute—he looked jus' like a lil' chipmunk! An' T—*Tyrell*—he was so *hilarious*, honey. *Oooh*—he jus' be steady *readin'* everybody, *all* the time! But…he'd be steady *slavin'* too, girl—like he was runnin' outta days. Anyway, he told me to bring my nursin' school friends 'round after our last finals, so I did. An' then he picked up the tab for *all* a us, girl—an' told me he was *real proud* a me…an', kept callin' me '*momma*'. Girl. Don't you know, two weeks after that, he called himself up an' dyin' in a car accident on the highway—on the way to *work*? Girl. *Oooh*—I'm a tell you, that jus' about killed me! Wish you coulda met him, girl. Nita keep tellin' me there's some other waiter there with his same name, an' I always say, 'mm-*hm*—that's probably T, still there—wise an' crackin' wise an' pickin' up shifts an' whatnot, *hahahahahaha* ! *Oooh*—feel like I'm fixin' to cry now. *Oooh*. So, uh…anyway girl—I was jus' hangin' out, havin' lunch wit' some friends a mine before graduation—"

"From nursing school, with honors," Juanita interjected, smiling as she had throughout Georgina's recounting. Juanita's hands had been unconsciously resting, clasped, on her belly. Reaching over, she tapped Georgina on the knee to nudge her into speaking about her other self—her other hand remaining gently on her abdomen. P.V.'s arms were shaking and prickled to every pore with shocks of goose pimples—hairs at each pucker raised, frozen, on end—inner spirit taking the strands of Georgina's story to complete its days-before revelation to her about Tyrell—Sterling. She glanced over at Georgina, features splayed-out surprised—not at Georgina's accolades, but at her café pre-tale. But Georgina winced, seeming to mildly mistake P.V.'s expression for dumbfound about her accomplishments, as she launched into the rest of her recollection.

"Sho did! An' I had graduated way early from college—with honors there, too, before that. An' I was at that nursing school on a *full scholarship*, girl. Ain' not a damn thang wrong wit' my head, honey! But...not like I do that now, though—I raise this whole tribe a chil'ren me an' D got now, you know? An' I like it that way, so far. But ain't nothin' wrong wit' my head. Okay, so, anyway—we's jus' hangin' out at the coffee shop, when...the door swung open to the kitchen, an' I saw all dese mens—male chefs—just a crammed up, sweaty an' slavin', honey. In this tiny, lil' kitchen! An' the ones I seen was all black—an' I mean jet black an' *glistenin'*, girl—wit' these white, white aprons an' all kinds a chef hats on. One was bendin' an' gittin' stuff out an oven, a couple of them was cookin' an' fryin' up on the stove, some was farther back cuttin' up stuff an' arrangin' thangs...I hadn' never seen anythang like it. An' somebody forgot to shut the door, so I don't know *what* got into me, but I jus' a stood up right where I was—right there—an' was jus' a starin' at 'em. An' a couple of 'em felt me watchin' at 'em, I guess, an' was jus' a starin' an' grinnin' back..."

"Was one of them Deacon?" P.V. blurted out, abruptly pausing her intake of more sangria in mid-air. Georgina laughed out a flat '*ha!*' that bubbled over into squeaking giggles breathed into her fist. Juanita's tandem giggles were prefaced by a protracted, involuntary snort. P.V. glanced to-and-fro at their glee-filled faces, hungry for instant clarification.

"*Hahahahaha*," Georgina managed, chuckling. "*Girrrl*—Deacon *try*, but outside a grillin' an' barbecuin' thangs, he cain't cook on any indoor surface to save his natural self, let alone to save me an' them ten kids we got—'less it got grill bars on it."

"*Ten kids?*" P.V. exclaimed incredulously, searching for exactly where on the woman's slight, sinewy-muscled frame manifested traces of bearing an entire brood.

"*Girrrl*, yeah—*ten* kids! An' I had all ten at home, wit' a midwife! *Girrrl*—we got started *early*, honey!" she replied, smiling proudly, sweeping at the air nonchalantly for emphasis.

"I call them 'The Villagers'," Juanita chimed in, elegantly popping a pita slice, pointy tip dotted carefully with P.V.'s creamy, homemade yogurt dip, into her mouth. "Y'all *do* have your own world over there, chica."

"*Huh*—right? An' trust, P.V.—Nita know the only folk who can cook up on a stove *in* that world are me an' Baby Seven," she laughed out loud again, Juanita joining her in profuse giggles.

"Baby Seven?" P.V. queried, cocking her head to the side and furrowing her brow, as she inserted a dainty pinch of a patty into her mouth.

"Girl, yes—*told* you I got ten kids, right? Well—I ran outta names an' energy 'round the seventh one, honey. So me an' Deacon agreed to jus' name him 'Seven'. Came out breach birth to boot, honey—like he was jus' ready to step up in this world an' start runnin' thangs. So that was an emergency call to the ob/gyn by my midwife, let me tell *you*, girl. Big Momma—that's my midwife—was *beside* herself, child. An' e'er since he could creep, I swear he been all up in my kitchen—spice cabinet, fridge, stove, pantry—an' e'erythang in there, honey. Now, he stand right up next to me on a lil' step-stool, helping me mix thangs an' whatnot—that is, when he not busy takin' e'erythang in the pantry an' spice cabinet out an' puttin' it in his mouth, child. *Girrl*—had to call at him one day in there, I says, 'Boy! Watch yo'self—that's *horseradish*, honey!' *Hahahahaha*—he didn' even flinch—that's my little man! *Shoooooot*—anythang happen to Baby

Seven, I jus' be *beside* myself, honey. Like the Good Book say—he my cornerstone, girl!"

P.V., turning over Georgina's words and world in her head, attempted a smile—but it remained a lift only at the corners of her mouth, tiny lips pursed and cast downwards. She watched at Juanita, who was still nodding her head vigorously—as she had throughout Georgina's recountings—and wondered about motherhood and wivery. Somewhere within, gnawing at her, was that it seemed one had to—on some level—get past the point of being exactly like a child to have one. She felt herself press forward, profoundly through the thighs, on the spotted footstool, almost involuntarily inclining to hear more. And then her mouth pulled her brain out of its inwardness, before she could meet up with it to speak. "Wow...cool. You're—that's like, awesome. So...you were telling me how you and Deacon met?"

"*Oh*...yeah..." Georgina began, a tad bewildered at the quality of P.V.'s reply. "...So...anyways, girl, I jus' stood right there in the restaurant, watchin' at all these mens busy in the kitchen—who was watchin' at *me*. An' then Deacon comes up behind me outta nowhere—all dressed to the nines like church on Sunday, honey. An' he says to me, 'uh, Miss—can I aks you a question?' An I says, 'yassir—you surely *can*'. An he says, 'uh, can I aks—what is you lookin' at up in there?' An' he pointed to the kitchen. An' I jus' *laughed*—'cause I couldn' even really put my finger on it. An' I says, 'well, I 'on't even know. But whatever it is, I jus' ain' never seen nuthin' like it before.' An' he jus' laughed—an' next thang I know, girl, we was courtin' an' carryin' on like old married folk!" P.V. half-chuckled, nodding to herself, soul smarting over how sweet that first meeting of Georgina and Deacon's was, compared to her and Rodney's own.

Giggling, Juanita added, "An' that's not even the best part." P.V. looked sharply at Georgina, eyebrows up, eager to know more.

"Well…" Georgina said demurely, looking down at the samosa in her hands. In a flash, she shoved a large portion of a corner of it into her mouth, eyes widening instantaneously as the unfamiliar sting of a robust curry exploded across her tongue. She jumped up—frantically, shakily, pouring herself some ice water from the dewy pitcher, spilling dimes and quarters of the liquid onto the silver serving tray. "Ooooh—*girl*! These *good*, but they *hot*! *Ooooh*! Um, you make these yo'self?"

"Oh! Yeah, I did—sorry!" P.V. was chagrined. Blushing and rising, she grappled for the bowl of accompaniment yogurt and shoved it into Georgina's free hand. "Eat this, *quick*—like, it'll like, help cool things off way faster. *Oh*…so, so, *sorry*! Um, I keep—I keep like, forgetting not to make curry like I'm feeding my Mum and Dad or something."

"Naw—it's okay, girl! Though, I think I seen Glory for a minute— *hahahahaha*—but it's okay! An' what's more important, these *good*, girl! Hot like a cattle brand—*hahahahaha*—but *good*! You should start a caterin' business on the side or somethin', honey! They 'bout the only people still makin' decent money nowadays, regardless—'cause e'erybody still be plannin' they weddings an' baby showers, but a lot a folk still ain' tryin' to cook it all themselves, no matter *what*, honey,"

"An' *quinceañeras,* too—but we cook!" Juanita added.

"Giiiirl, yes—an' *quinceañeras* for all *time*, child," Georgina agreed. "Somethin' to think about. Shoot—Juanita girl, you should help her. Y'all could start a new business or somethin'." She shot Juanita a knowing glance as, trying to quell the residual burn, she patted at her chest, and then shoveled another large dollop of yogurt into her mouth.

P.V. laughed a little first, hollowly, uncomfortably, nodding with a pride in her cooking—but also with the uncertainty regarding the days ahead for her own household. If it were all to remain the same—the same as it had downspiritedly, hopelessly, violently been—she could not speak for it, nor for herself. She felt a wave of sadness encircle a point somewhere deep in the flesh of her heart and flow through it. She answered, mind still reeling. "Thanks, um, but—I...um...I just like, cook like, just *because* these days. I mean, I was like, cooking for Rod and me—but..." She paused, looking down at her hands, chiefly the left one. Encircling the ring finger was a thick and decadent, winking platinum wedding band. "...He stays out late now, um, so...you know...like, he's trying to network some more, so he can maybe find the in on a job...or something like that. So like, for cooking, it's just...you know...it's just me."

Georgina and Juanita exchanged knowing glances with each other, shifting uneasily in their chairs. They knew well best, as fledgling friends, to avoid tapping further just then into the night whereabouts of Rodney.

"Oh *well*, girl," Georgina uttered soothingly. "We should all jus' have a dinner party in here or somethin'—maybe invite some folks. I'm always up for some grown folk company, havin' to deal wit' my ten lil' angels all day—an' I could bring a dish! We *all* could. I know how it is when you like to cook, but don't really have nobody to cook for. I got a sister like that, an' she jus' about as plumb miserable as she can be 'til she come to our house at Thanksgiving an' Christmas, an' git her cook on for e'erybody an' they momma."

"Right?" Juanita agreed eagerly. "Hey—an' about the dinner party, maybe we could do it every other week—like on a Saturday or something. Yeah, everybody could bring something—an' *someone*, like friends, husbands, wives...It could be jus' be a great way to get to know new people, an'...you know...it might be good for business, too."

"Now, Deacon an' Beau won't we able to be to go if we do it on Saturdays though," Georgina inserted. "Nita know they be playin' knock-down serious Texas Hold 'Em poker e'ery Saturday at my house, wit' they other male friends—rain or shine—like a straight up clockwork."

Hahahahaha! An' they be playin' for *money*, honey—they *mens* about that—so they don't even be *late* to the game. But...you know what? Shoot—e'en if it is, I ain' gon' let that stop anythang—'specially if it's about raising up new clients, too. I'll pass roun' Deacon's business cards in a heartbeat. You know all our household money got to go to our lil' tribe a ten! Thangs was just fine a few years ago, but nowadays? Uh-uh. As it is, it look like I'm a have to go back to my nursin' career—maybe work for a nursin' temp agency a few hours here an' there a somethin'—or find out a way to do it full-time. An' then the question is—who gon' watch my kids then? 'Cause we sure can't afford to pay nobody. *Mm*! Jus' a whole other mess a wrinkles, girls. Hear me goin' on—P.V. you so quiet—what you think?"

"Um—sure, yeah. Like, that sounds like a lot of fun, actually," P.V. replied softly, far away with a mind wrapped around so much of the recent past and all of the bits of information that just flew into her. Inside, she was brightening in slow, tiny degrees at the thought of having a spaceful of dinner guests every other week. Dinner parties could perhaps be the start of having a life like what she left with her sorors and bridesmaids in California—jaunting off to cooking classes and vineyards, luxuriating in good-friend weekends away, and now, escaping the raking touch of Rodney and his unapologetic absences. Building business in a strange place, at a strange time, was an absolute necessity, but the truth was that she kept holding out an overriding, unfounded hope for the camaraderie and cruising-whilst-learning portion of her old California life. Her mind was sometimes just at spinning its wheels on the idea of returning to the waves and sun, and finding a way to succeed there again—despite the market. Something in her wanted to just go through the motions now—and have fun where she could—and then run back to Cali, create a compelling reason to leave. But, visibly shaking the dreams out of her head for a moment, she brought the conversation back to that flag that had sat straight up in her mind when it was raised. "So, um—what was the best part? Like, Juanita was saying—about you and Deacon?"

"Best part—oh yeah, girrrl! We had a *sex* problem!!" Georgina replied gleefully.

"A....*sex* problem?" P.V. was now all ears and face turning to frown, nervous as to what was to be said next.

"Yeah—the problem was that we couldn' have any sex!" Georgina tossed out, dissolving into giggles with Juanita. Seeing a look of confusion and an odd pain flash across P.V.'s face, Georgina struggled desperately to compose herself and continue.

"Yeah...uh, see, girl—Deacon from Oklahoma way. He real big on church an' you know, respect an' thangs like that. An' I mean, so am I. I'm an Okie too, but I was raised *right* up here in Dallas—we was *always* in the church. Anyway, we found out later that Deacon was kin to my godmother, an' that—get this—we all atten' the same church! We got a *big* congregation—*way* up in the 1000's, girl. So ain' no surprise I jus' ain' never met him, 'cause I was goin' to the early service, an' I thought I knew who all was my kinfolk roun' here, anyway. Didn' know any other Okies was up this way. So anyway, when we started courtin', we started attendin' the same service—we do to this very day—an' outta respect, since we started seein' my godmother e'ery Sunday, well...we decided we was gon' wait—you know, to have sex. I mean, you know how them old ones be knowin' all yo' business by jus' lookin' in yo' *eyes*, an' whatnot! Girrrl—the Spirit be *tellin'* on you! An' then, nex' thang you know, my *Momma* would find out, an' I'd have to hear 'bout myself *all over* ag'in, from *her*—an' I wasn' even *tryin'* ta go *there*, girl!"

"*Right?*" Juanita chirped, agreeing. P.V. looked at them both blankly, wishing for that problem back—of being without the sex, without that knowledge, without the realization of what else could be lurking behind a bedroom door. Georgina sensed the shift in her mood, and tried to encourage her back into smiling.

"*Girl*. Anyway—I was 19 an' Deacon was 18, an' needless to say, we *tried*, but we couldn't keep our hands off each other. We made it all the way to the night before our weddin', child—an' then got pregnant that *very night*. An' e'er since then, it's been the nonstop to the babymakin', honey—*hahahahahahaha*! But, shoo—girl, Nita the one who husband followed her all the way home."

Juanita laughed coyly, tossing her hair slightly, uptaking a sip of a truly golden iced tea infused with mango. "Yeah, chica—hey, *wow*! P.V., I *like* this *tea*—you *have* to give me the *recipe*! Gina wasn't kidding—dinner party—we *have* to do it, you know?"

"The *story*, girl," Georgina interjected.

"Oh, right—-sorry. Um, well—Beau wasn't playing, you know?" Juanita began. P.V. leaned forward, swiftly, neatly closing her silverware parallel together in a single sweep. She was both eager to hear the story and prophylactically jealous of it, saddened by it—knowing that again, hers could not compare. But she heard herself say, 'really?' and 'what happened?' to the conversation's air.

Juanita chuckled, flipping a lock of hair back. "*Ohhh*—we were both 18, an' I had this job at the college. I used to take the bus to work, an' Beau would like, be there everyday, sitting there with me. An' then one day, he asked me to marry him—an' then he asked me out. *Hahahaha*! It was hilarious—an' so *sweet*! He's jus' so sweet! It was jus' so—I mean, him with those big eyes jus' looking at me, like he was looking at his queen or something! An' then—get this—he confessed that, like, he actually had a truck an' everything, that he was only at the bus stop to be with me, an' see who I really was, an' where I lived! Oh..." she paused, slightly fiddling around in her purse and producing, from its highly compartmentalized depths, her smartphone. "...This is Beau," she said, clicking to his picture onscreen and handing the phone to P.V. "He sells insurance—you know, auto-home-life—for a major carrier. Wait—I'll give you his card. We like to take care of our friends! An'—feel free to tell other people you know about him. He works so hard, but nowadays...you know—he could sure use more business."

"O-*kay*?" Georgina agreed. "It sho ain't like e'erybody buyin' up insurance or new, American cars the way they used to. Deacon an' Beau be talkin' 'bout that! They say it ain't never been like this for them before. An' me an' Nita *know* that's true. Gon' take a long, long time to git us up outta the mess we all been put up in—but I *know* I voted in the right brutha for the job!"

P.V. examined the photo. Beau was white, and a stretching, slender man with spiky, brownish-blonde hair. He had intensely seafoam-blue, profoundly expressive, eyes; and a smattering of light brown freckles all about the top of his nose. He was white tee shirt and jeans sitting in a chair, cowboy-booted feet up—long-necked beer in one hand, the other resting on his taut belly. And he was mouth open and smiling, kind eyes beaming out from a visually alert, active spirit. That picture too, hurt P.V. to the core, as he was—similar to Deacon—noticeably happy, in love and loving, and radiating the all of it out. His face was wearing a fun, a togetherness, and a stay-put loyalty. P.V. realized just then that their cell phone pictures, and her own, truly said so much—and that the images would tell and tell and tell again, and that there was no hiding from the big truths they squeezed out onto the tiny, pin dots of pixel.

"Happiest white man you e'er did meet, girl," Georgina offered. "I go over they house an' they be *all up* on the porch—Beau wit' his head up in Nita's lap, an' him jus' a sunnin' an' grinnin', *hahahahaha*! I always be sayin' to her, '*Girrrrl*—what you *put* on that man?' He jus' transfixed to the altogether, honey. *Hahahahahahaha*! But Nita, girl—tell her the *rest* a the story." P.V. looked curiously up at Juanita.

"W-well, yeah," Juanita stammered. "*Chica...*" she sighed, shaking her head. "I mean—he comes from one of those families, you know? Where like, I mean—they'll speak, say 'good morning' an' stuff like that—but..." she paused, searching for a genteel way to speak the thing into the open.

"They don' like Blacks *or* Mexicans, girl—an' a course you know, Juanita's both, honey," Georgina neatly finished for her.

"Oh!" P.V.'s face was all raised to her eyebrows, shocked at what Juanita had wed into, had on some level accepted. "Like, I mean—how..."

"Well, you know...we jus' started dating. An' well, I mean—for awhile, maybe nobody knew about it. I didn' say anything. But...I mean people find out, you know? I mean, Mami—she knew—an' all my family did. An, I mean, Mami's hus...my Dad—he died in a car accident on the highway when I was eleven, so...but I mean, *his* family found out, *too*, so...so, you know—Beau's family *had* to know, somehow—you know? But...surprisingly, nobody said anything. Not to me, not to Beau. I thought maybe his family didn' because they thought he would jus', you know, get it out of his system—sometimes people like that *think* like that, you know? But...I mean—in hindsight, that wasn't it."

"Wh—like, did they...did they come to the wedding?" P.V. was body forward, brow wrinkling, instantly awake and intrigued at the response.

"Well, after he like, really proposed, I said, you know—'how are we going to do this', you know? 'You know how your family is.' An' he just said he's 18 an' he's a grown man now, an' could do whatever he wants—an' tha' what he wants is to marry me, an' tha' as far as he was concerned with them, that tha's jus' how it was gonna be. I was like, 'okay'—but I was really, really nervous about it. I mean—I didn' know *what* they were going to say—or *do*, you know? So, then he told his parents—an' they just said they already knew. Tha's it. Then they told him to go talk to his Uncle Jed—an' I mean, his Uncle Jed's from the part of the family that's like, from way across deep South, but he owns a Texas barbecue restaurant out where we're from. An' when he went to go talk to Jed at his house, he was outside—barbecuing a whole mess of like, hogs' ribs an' some whole hogs, on some of his like, mega pits, you know? An', I mean—he saw Beau out of the corner of eye, you know? But he didn' say nothing to him. So, Beau jus' started telling him what he told his parents. An' his uncle didn' even *look* at him when he was talking—just kept, you know, feeding ribs to the grill an' turning them. An' then, when he was finished talking, his uncle didn' even turn around. He jus' said, 'that's what you want?' An' Beau said, 'Yessir'. An' he said, 'if that's what you want, it's fine by me—pretty-lookin' gal—I ain' gon' talk you outta it. You jes' tell me what y'all wanna eat an' what time y'all 'spect folks ta be where'. An' tha' was it! An' I mean, Jed cooked *all* the food for our wedding reception—an' it was *amazing*, you know? The beef was so like, tender—jus' falling apart when you looked at it, an' the smoke, it was jus' right…I mean, *mira* it was so good, he had to cook tha' with *love* or something, okay? An' we had it at *his restaurant*, too! An' I mean—they were like, *all there*, you know? *All* Beau's family—pretty much, anyway. It was like, *wild*—you know?"

P.V., touched and intrigued, thought deeply for moments, idly tracing a teardrop of condensation falling quickly down the side of her frosty goblet-full of sangria. She watched the bright red liquid settle against the rind of the whole pieces of citrus fruit, as they rested in the glass. Her fave part of the drink was sucking down the sweet-sour flesh steeped in the wine at its end in the vessel. But—she wasn't nearly there to the bottom. She sighed and wondered for a moment why life always seemed that way lately—taking so long to get to the innermost part. That part, she reasoned within herself, would remarkably change, advise, her.

"But what do they call you?" she blurted out. Juanita and Georgina exchanged quick glances with each other, looking back at P.V., eyebrows raised and wordlessly querying.

"Wh—" Georgina, alarmed, began to inquire.

P.V. shocked at her own utterance, stared wide-eyed at her. "Um—Deacon—what does he call you? Like, your name...does he have um-um, like, nicknames for you?"

"Oh. Uh...well *yeah*, girl," Georgina replied, casting another curious, questioning glance at Juanita. "Uh, well...I mean—he call me 'Georgina' sometimes, but that's only when we goin' over the household budget." They all laughed, her levity temporarily breaking the odd tension.

"An' I mean, he do jus' call me 'Gina', too. But for the most part—he so sweet—he be callin' me 'Ma'am', since when he firs' met me at that café he called me 'Miss'. Or sometimes he call me 'Mother', on account a how I take good care a him an' all them chil'rens we got."

"That's so cool," P.V. replied quietly, inner cogs turning, eyes fleeting a look out at the short-depth, concrete balcony. "Um, like—what about you, Juanita? Like, um, what does Beau call you?"

"Uh...well," Juanita began, glancing at Georgina. "He calls me 'Juanita' or 'Nita'. Or, you know, 'Honey'—stuff like that." Then she chuckled a little, placing a lock of hair behind one ear. "But sometimes, he also calls me 'Layla', like that song—remember tha' one? He says it's just like the couple in the song—that tha's how he feels about me."

To Juanita and Georgina's amazement, P.V. immediately rose up from the dalmatian-patterned footstool—perfectly and perfunctorily, as if hearing a dog whistle—and began clearing their plates and the remains of the savories, ferrying them smoothly to the kitchen. By rights, it was partly almost an instinctive process, something she had done as a very young girl for her parents, back in Miami—and had been doing for Rodney, until almost recently, every night. But her mind was also screaming at her to rise up, that everyone else—her parents, Georgina, Juanita—had better love backstories than hers, better working married lives than hers. And it shrieked at her too, that all of *their* walls heard their *real* names, as well as their little, loving, pet names for each other. *Their* men could even cook, even if it *was* relegated to that which was the traditionally male—the grill, the barbecue—and there was something she thoroughly respected about that. And—their men had jobs. Too, it was clear—crystal unto their pictures—that those men had passionate, to-the-marrow-and–beyond-it love for their wives. They were men and women—and in their couplehood, they were real. In all of a 360, they had operational, seemingly non-dysfunctional, age-appropriate lives.

She, conversely, for all intents and purposes, was married to a frat boy—a Peter who grew too well up and then regressed, and was now violent and behaving as if he didn't ever know what being grown up truly meant. Her stomach started to sear, with the resurgent flash of acid lapping up at the injustice of it all—at the difference between what *she* had received in marriage and the bounty of marital gifts that had been bestowed on everyone else. It then occurred to her as her foot crossed the doorless kitchen threshold—tiny fingers multitasking, hands laden at all angles with dishes, silverware, bowls—that the only thing all of their marriages perhaps had in common was women conjuring up amenable menus, filling up the table with food, and then clearing away the magic when the dinner show was over.

P.V. returned to a furtively whispering-together Georgina and Juanita. She was bearing effortlessly, unthinkingly, an almost exactly mirror-reflective silver coffee tureen, and balancing teaspoons on china teacups and saucers etched with a vibrant, red and metallic gold lattice pattern.

"Uh...P.V., girl—since you asked...what, uh...what does *Rodney* call you?" Georgina queried, exchanging glances with Juanita again.

P.V. silently, carefully, set down the cups and saucers in front of both women. Bending, she poured the rich, dark roast slowly into each, from a height first then lower, closer—measuring to perfection. But missing were her own teacup, saucer, spoon, coffee. She thought for moments, and realized in that instant that of the two, 'boozhe' had long since left the unpretty, re-baptizing picture. And so her remaining classification stood by itself, so plainly, so knifingly used—so alone. "Wifey," she whispered, staring at her ring hand on the tureen, staring out at a supposed everything that had been rendered, day by day, night by night, a nothing. "Just...*wifey.*"

She counted the waters, missing the ocean, and found her quiet in the river, lakes, creeks on which she had, without being asked, compromised. She even found a solace in a surprising tributary off of one of the highways, floating with trees and sometimes a few ducks—but as she drove past, it was too quickly there and then gone. In jaunts to Fort Worth and Weatherford and beyond to assist clients, she saw hay and hay around bales of hay, and from miles around, cows lazily grazing on high and low green hills. But, in her increasing anxiety and depression, the sun shone too much upon her—like a big, in-bounding ball, like stadium lighting bearing down full onto the face—incessantly, at all hours of the day. It was as if the sun were urging her to spill her secrets, attempting to draw out from her the mounting piles of pain. These were things she could not say to Georgina and Juanita—they were all too new to her world, so she dared not risk interrupting whatever perfection was forming with them as friends. But, she couldn't tell her sorors and bridesmaids back in California either, being of a disposition too shy and ashamed to relay to any one of them what terrifying things Rodney had, in the Texas nights, wrought upon her flesh, mind, soul.

Oddly, seemingly to make up for drunkenly mauling her in the bedroom on the weeknights that he did appear—and for a Thanksgiving day that P.V. unexpectedly spent by herself blankly watching television and eating chips—Rodney began to insist on 'cooking' dinners for her. During the latter portion of those nights, he still made himself scarce speedily and altogether, and when he 'cooked' in the early evenings for her, it consisted of tossing budget t.v. dinners into the microwave, and washing it down with beer. They all looked so uncomfortably plastic to P.V., all of the various and sundry, cheap microwave boxes lying on the table, counters, trash bin. Their packaging was like all things commercially assigned to childhood—too iridescent, primary, portioned. The food seemed much of the same to her. It was as if he were feeding her edible toys, junk so bright—symbols, unbeknownst to her, of what his own inner world had become.

And the principles of radiation itself equally began to wear upon P.V. The microwave meals were overdone by Rodney to begin with—as he seemed to have lost his entire sense of focus and timing—and full of nothing but recharged chemicals. So, it seemed sadly natural that they were, further, place-set and consumed in a similarly sucking and dynamic silence. She could hardly look at or talk to him, for fear he would snap as he often did, and haul her fighting off to the bedroom. So, one Saturday, she thought she would try at cooking for him again, despite everything. She loaded up at the farmer's market, an out of town dairy farm, a local butcher shop, and a nearby fish market, little arms laden with several of her organic hemp grocery bags from her life back in Cali. As she opened the door to the rented condo, the wheeing sound of the microwave jutted out to her, accompanied by the everywhere smells of mingled, muffled whatever.

"Hey," P.V. called out flatly to the air, disappearing quickly around the corner and into the kitchen, her bags piled to their tops with fresh produce, dairy items, fish, and just-butchered meat.

"*Heeyy*," Rodney replied drunkenly from deep within the suite, mocking her.

Perceiving his mood and feeling a wave of nausea instinctively rising in her throat, P.V. washed her hands and walked quickly, bravely, out of the kitchen, straight on the diagonal into the corner dining room. Rodney was stilt-long legs cocked well up on the table, 1/3 of a bottle of gin at his ankle-crossed, naked feet. His hands were loosely clutching their black checkbook, and were resting just slightly above his crotch. He jealously surveyed her attire. She was clad head to-to-toe in power red and gold, complete with coordinating, square-heeled black patent leather flats with gold accents at the heel juncture. It was an outfit he recognized, that she had before, but the seeing of her in it—with the knowledge that she had a place to wear it—further enraged him.

"*Heyyy*, da bitch!" he sassed, eyes blazing into hers. Waving the checkbook loopily, and deliberately eyeing her outfit again, he snapped, "Well, ain't *you* da bitch." She glanced at him and then at the floor, something within her whispering at her to keep her tongue.

"*15 grand?*" he cried out, flashing the checkbook out in front of him and paging wildly through it. P.V. persisted in saying nothing—waiting, holding her breath.

"I mean—when was you gon' tell me about da *15 grand*, Wifey?" Rodney was nostrils flared, voice shrill, and eyes like headlight high beams—too hot and radiating out. P.V. remained still, silent, increasingly unsteady on her legs on the faux wood floor.

"I mean, what you *sell*, Wifey—mutha fuckin' *oil?*"

P.V. cleared her throat, apprehensively adjusting a lapel, eyes darting everywhere. "Um..my-my parents thought we could probably use…it's like, just their way of…of taking care of…" she incompletely pleaded. And then she sighed, all of a sudden thoroughly exhausted. "It's…it's just like a housewarming gift, Roddie. Just…it's just like that."

He glared at her, eyes flickering from within a frozen, grey-overcast countenance. "Uh-*huh*. You just said about *three mutha fuckin' different things*, Wifey. So which one is it? Huh? Nah, nah, nah. Y'heard? *Nah*. So, *translation*, I guess I'm not a *man* in dey eyes now—is dat it? Huh? Can't take care a my own household, *huh*? Can't take care a m'house, so, yo' foreign, rich-ass mommy an' daddy got ta step in an' *save* the mutha fuckin' *day*, huh? Dat it? 'Cause you ain't really married to a *man*—is you, huh? Dat about right? Married to a mutha fuckin' *boy*—boy orphan an' shit—who can't take care a his mutha fuckin' shit, *or* you. Huh, Wifey? *Dat* it? Dat what dey think? Dat what *you* think? Dat about right? Hah?"

P.V. was enveloped by her own mindful absence of sound, looking down and away intermittently like a child being chastised. She was staring every so often at a spot for comfort—just beyond her low-heeled work shoes—at a particularly defined, manufactured wormhole on the faux dark wood floor. But from the bubble, she heard herself reply to him quietly, begging under the bright line of his anger. "Roddie—like, I mean, the market's already getting worse, Roddie. It's—it's like…that's like…*everywhere*. And I mean—I have to get deals and then, like, wait for them to close— you know that. And that—that just, like, takes time…especially—especially now. I mean—I'm gonna like…they have a service where you—you can get an advance on your commissions and, I mean, I'm like, gonna do that, but, I mean…I figured—my parents figured—well…that like, *until* like, *whenever*, that we'd…need…um, like, *help*. I mean, it's just—they're just…like, they're just trying to help us, Roddie."

"Oh, uh-*huh*—trying to *help*," Rodney snapped. "Two mutha fuckin' Third World people tryin' ta help *my* ass—all up in my own *country* an' shit. *Huh*. An' I see you think dat mutha fuckin' entitles you to be movin' money all aroun' the show too, huh? Puttin' money all up in da savings account an' shit. So, basically, *you* ain't really ~~married~~—or like I said, yo' *parents* think you married to some mutha fuckin' *boy*, huh? An' *you* think you da *woman* now—since you da only one wit' a *job*. So you and yo' rich-ass mommy and daddy jus' think *you* da one s'posed to be runnin' things now—inclusive of all our finances an' shit, huh? I see how it is. I see. *Huh*. So—when was you gon' tell me, Wifey? Huh? When was you gon' tell me that you da mutha fuckin' *woman* now?"

P.V. looked away, all the words crashing in like wild, imaginary birds—sharp-beaked, and full of ire. They were everywhere, pecking relentlessly at her from the air and then jabbing their way into her head, psyche. "I never said that," she whispered.

"*Oh—ohh*. You ain't never *said* dat? You ain't never *had* to say dat, Wifey. 'Til now, huh? An' you 'on't *have* to say dat now, Wifey. It's how— it's how you apparently mutha fuckin' think it *is*. All behind my back. It's how you mutha fuckin' *actin'*, bitch! *Pshht*. It's even how you *walkin'* an' shit nowadays. Like you—like you *mutha fuckin'* tryin' ta *own* da place. Like you little Miss *Thang*."

"You don't like me, do you?" P.V. blurted out. She instantly wished she could retrieve the question, reel it yanking back from the whirling sea of molecules.

"*No*, I guess I fuckin' *don't*, Boozhe—Wifey," Rodney snapped again, eyes full of liquid. "I mean, *not really*. *Huh*. An' since you think you Miss *Thang* now, I guess I *definitely* mutha fuckin' *don't*."

She stared at him, dumbfounded, the breath sucked from her belly, lungs, mouth. And nowhere was there replacement oxygen, just nowhere.

He grinned darkly up at her, shaking the gin bottle and downing another swig. Capping it carefully, he added, "But—you Miss Thang everywhere but where you *should* be, *ain't* you, Wifey? I don't give a fuck about you cooking food for me—I'd rather be out doin' stuff—I always been that way anyway, an' you *know this*. But I *do* damn sure like ta git *fucked*. An' all you fuckin' do is cry an' cry an' fight an' lay dere. Got to *force* you to suck a dick—an' everything else, for dat matter. I mean, *damn*, Wifey—can't even suck a good *dick*. Didn't dem *sorors* teach yo' ass how ta suck a good *dick*? I mean, how'd you get past *Rush* week, Boozhe? *Dang*! I know you was a *virgin* den, but *damn*. You hadn't done *shit*, had you? Thought you Caribbean girls was supposed ta know how ta cook *and* suck dick an' fuck an' git pregnant an' shit. Why da fuck I git stuck wit' one who *cain't—fuck*, dat is? I mean, had ta teach you *every* fuckin' thing about fuckin'—an' den you cryin' an' hollerin' an' strugglin' like somebody rapin' you. Ain't nobody *rapin'* you, Wifey. You jus' *fragile*. Jus' *fragile* an' shit." P.V. felt rooted to the faux floor boards, bolted down on half-substance, the world spinning at dizzying ellipses all around her.

"An' while we're on *dat* subject," Rodney continued, standing and swaying at a walk towards her, "What you need to do as *soon* as mutha fuckin' *possible* is ta find yo'self an ob/gyn an get yo'self a diaphragm a somethin' like dat." P.V., terrified at his forward motion, immediately began taking steps slowly back, brow wrinkled, hands out to protest.

"Don't look at me like dat. Ain't you ever heard a no barrier methods? I mean, bein' a virgin before you married don' have nuthin' to do wit' health class an' shit. Wasn't dat mutha fuckin' mandatory at yo' high school in Florida an' shit? What da fuck was dey teachin' y'all down dere, anyway?" P.V. shook her head, half-glancing behind her to avoid tripping over the ringing, occasional furniture.

"Come 'ere, Wifeeey—little Miss Thaaang. Come 'eeere," Rodney cooed suddenly, grinning wickedly, widening his eyes purposefully, fixing them on hers.

"I don't want to," she bleated, the sound of her retreating gait quicker, audible against the floor. She glanced back again, a sick feeling washing over her as she realized that instead of pivoting *past* the kitchen, toward the corner that began the hallway to the exit, to the unit door, she had treaded backwards—one tile *into* it.

"What you mean you don't *want* to, *Wifey*? Seriously—you *best* git *over* here," he warned, smile disappearing from his face.

"No."

"No? *No*? *Huh*. You *best* be *playin'* girl—'cause I 'on't got *time* for dis *shit*."

"I can't—I..I have my period," P.V. lied, looking at him sidelong with doe eyes, holding her breath—hoping the excuse would land, lock, fix. She crossed her arms tightly across her chest as she lunged sideways, to try to exit the kitchen opening. But in one easy stride and sneering triumphantly, he caught up with her, shooting out a seemingly endless arm to corral her back into the space. As she retreated up deeper into the belly of the kitchen, he gazed unwaveringly down and into her, searching her eyes.

"*Ohhh*—see. *I* see. *Huh*. You playin' a dangerous *game* right now, Wifey," Rodney said heavily, voice steady and floating threateningly to her. P.V. felt her bottom hit the edge of the sink, the wave of nausea—with a hopelessness—returning. She crossed her arms once more, across her shallowly respiring chest. Rodney effortlessly bridged the gap between them again, and leaning fully against her, began to open and shut the upper cabinet doors well above her head. He slowly and deliberately patted the rear portion within each one carefully, as if searching for something. A jolt of fear, wet, metallic and salty, sprang into the back of P.V.'s throat, watering the sides of her tongue.

Without looking at her, Rodney sighed, and dropped his voice even further, just above a whisper, still patting the back of one cabinet. "Ahhh, Wifey. Don't be tryin' ta play dat game. Not wit' me. Ain't nobody gon' win wit' dat game today—an' *I'm y'man.* So, I *know* you an' shit, 'cause I *trained* you an' shit. An' dat shit right dere dat you tryin' ta *play* wit' me older dan e'ery earthly muh fucka combined—an' you oughta *know* dat an' furthermore—you know you ain't *like* dat an' shit." P.V.'s insides had already jumped, all flesh, into her throat and were straining out. She felt the air pressure as if weighty and dropping around her, pulse pounding the fear up into her ears. She kept her arms crossed and contracted, tight about her chest. Rodney began leaning, increasingly, into her in increments, the force and mass of his body pushing her painfully further into the jut of the counter.

He dropped his hands down, placing them on either side of her on the counter, and curved his body over and around, lips hovering just about her ear. And he whispered to her: "*See—it's jus' dat you don't know nothin' about dat shit, and den gon' mess around wit' me an' get yo' ass hurt an' hard fucked today, Wifey—when dat shit coulda all been avoided by yo' ass jus' comin' correct, an' lettin' yo' man ha' some wit'out protest. An' by da way—dat, Wifey, is how bitches get dey asses hurt. So don't ever be tryin' ta game me, Wifey—'cause I know all about dem chick tricks. Besides—clearly ain't too hard to check whether you havin' yo' period or not, an' you know y'man crazy as hell—I'll check right here an' shit—right now. I mean—dat ain't no thing ta verify, 'specially behind closed doors an' shit. Dis is my crib—I can do what I want. An' you gon' wish I hadn't had ta do dat shit, Wifey. So use yo' mutha fuckin' head. Besides—dis da 2000's—all I got ta do is put yo' ass on one a dem four-periods-a-year birth control joints, like dey advertise on t.v., an den you'll be a four-periods-a-year havin' bitch. End a game—I win. But I wanna ha' some lil' men one day—so I 'on't jus' wanna be fuckin' wit' yo' endocrine system like dat an' shit. But you keep it the fuck up, Wifey—you try ta game me ag'in, an' you gon' be dat four-periods bitch—I straight up, mutha fuckin' guarantee you dat."*

Rodney stopped abruptly—and for want of something else to say or do, happened to glance up and around the depth of the kitchen. The heart of the boxy, u-shaped counter was packed to the under of the upper cabinets with fibrous grocery bags brimming with meat packages, celery, tomatoes and other produce. And he noted that P.V. had already begun to place some of the well-used hanging pots and pans on the stove. He looked back at her, taking in her increasingly saucer-wide eyes.

"Ya know, Wifey..." he began again, slowly, methodically, thinking it through as he uttered. He was forehead approaching to only inches away from hers, and eyes to eyes—gauging each flutter of her lashes and subtle fluctuation in her irises. "...What I think is muh fuckin' *hilarious* is dat I see da one place I *haven't* fucked you is up in dis muh fuckin' *kitchen*, an' *dat* is a muh fuckin' *oversight* on *my* part—an' I apologize *wholeheartedly* for *dat* shit." He grinned wide, teeth flashing as she flinched, and then moved his gaze and head back to her ear. "'Cause, I don't want you ta *feel* or *believe* for *one second*, Wifey, dat dere is someplace up in here or anywhere else dat I *won't* try ta fuck you. Fuck *try*. Fuck you—*period*. All I gotta do is pick yo' little ass up an' *fuck* you, 'cause I'm a grown ass man an' my ass is, well, way stronger dan *yo'* ass. Dat's just biology, Wifey—an' muh fuckin' *physics*. An' I *will* make *sure*—if we happen ta be in public, that ain't nobody gonna be aroun' ta say *shit* ta me about dat. *Now*, what I *do* know—aside from da fact dat you don't want me ta fuck you no more—which is *yo'* problem, not mine, 'cause I am gon' be fuckin' you *regardless*, so you gon' have ta *deal* wit' dat on yo' *own* time. Shit—talk ta yo' ol' friends wit' all dey so-called good advice an' *work* dat shit *out*, Wifey. What I *do* know, Wifey—what I *do* know, is dat *dis* mutha fucka—dis *kitchen*—dis like some kinda sacred space for you an' shit. Uh-*huh*. You got it all up in here like a goddamned *church* an' shit—an' I *see* dat now."

He pulled back around again to gauge her face. What had been 100% fear had been quickly replaced by something that he hadn't quite seen before. He began wracking his head at high speed inwardly, for what it was, and then it occurred to him that it was obstinacy, rebellion—defiance. Something he had said had raised the fight in her.

Rodney went to unbutton P.V.'s blouse, to test the limits of his newfound theory, but her hands flew up like quick little windmills, slapping his away. Her elbows were flying at his chest, body twisting to break free in every direction. He was immediately amused—laughing as he neatly caught up her little wrists to contain her. "*Oh*! *Whoa, whoa, whoa*! *Hahahahaha*," he shouted, chuckling. P.V., struggling against his grip, found that she was able to free a hand. So, he scooped up her entire torso—arms pinned to her sides with his vise-like hold—into his arms. "*Oooh*—she *seriously* don't want me ta fuck her all up in dis kitchen!" he exclaimed, still laughing, taunting her. She was exerting all of her tiny force against his seeming all-encompassing deadweight. "*Whoa, whoa*—*hahahahaha*—ah-*ight*. Ah-*ight*. Hold up a second, Wifey—hold up—*hahahahaha*," he uttered derisively. But P.V. had already shifted into a state of constant wrestle against his grasp.

"Hold *up*, Wifey—seriously. A'ight—a'*ight*!" Rodney repeated again, grin less prominent across his countenance. P.V. paused, eyes up and searching his—looking for a truth in ending, praying for cessation. "*Hahahahaha*—I can't *belie'* dis shit. A'ight, a'ight—I tell you what. I ain' gonna lie ta you—I'll fuck you *regardless*, but I can see you gon' make things difficult in dat department, an' I ain' actually in da *mood* for dat shit tonight. I *will* fuck you fightin', of course, mind you—but I jus' ain' in da mood for it tonight, so if I have ta do it, dat jus' gon' piss me off—an' a course, den dat's gon' be uh, so much worse for *you*. *Now*—I wanna fuck like it was back in da beginning. Like it was back in da day, Wifey. Like back in da day when you liked me—or some shit like dat. So..." He stood back a bit, smirking and staring at her from one eye to the other, still holding her fast. "...if you agree ta make me *believe* da shit tonight—don' jus' lay dere, fuck *back* like you wanna *do* dat shit—den *I* won't fuck you strugglin' up against me in dis muh fuckin' church-assed shrine of a kitchen you got yo'self up in here."

P.V. stopped moving, shock stopping her breath for a moment, nausea creeping in and fast again up into her throat. She looked around at all of her groceries—fresh and abundant, and colorific against the backdrop of her hemp farmer's market bags—and at the pristinely scrubbed broken-in copper pots and pans, and the clean, gleaming slats of dark, faux wood floor. "*Okay,*" she said quietly, surprisingly roughly, pushing at once forcefully against Rodney's locking grip. She felt profoundly sick, vomit up-running its sure way into her esophagus.

"Wiiith *gusto,* Wifey," Rodney cheerily warned, a mischief everywhere from his eyes to smirking lips.

"I said *okay.*" P.V. snapped.

Rodney laughed again, stunned at his own luck. And, releasing only one of her arms, relocated his grip to her wrist, and began to pull her out of the kitchen with him, taunting her as he strode. "*Hahahahaha—oh!* I can't *belie'* dis shit—all over a muh fuckin' *kitchen.* Might I say, Miss Wifey—I'm lookin' *forward* to yo' muh fuckin' *performance*—yes I *am,* ma'am. *Hahahahaha—oh! How* my wifey don' want nobody ta fuck her up in her muh fuckin' kitchen! *Oh! Hahahahahahaha.*"

"Wait." P.V. said firmly, stopping Rodney's pull at her body. "I have to put the meat away."

Rodney's flash of anger returned, and he began to twist her arm. "Don't you *press* your *luck,* Wifey."

"I said *okay*—just let me put the meat and dairy away, and I'll be in there."

Rodney peered down at her, and was relieved to find that amidst her sudden defiance, was a certain resignation—an acceptance of her fate. "A'ight, a'ight," he chuckled, nodding, relinquishing his grasp. "Hurry up— an' den git on back dere, Wifey. Don't *make* me come for you."

P.V. felt the tears falling out of each cell of her eyes, as she shakily placed the cartons of large, brown eggs; and vibrantly-labeled containers of newly-squeezed milk and tubs of fresh, creamy butter, into the spotless, stainless steel refrigerator. Her hands quivered again into the comforting, brisk air of the fridge, cupping and laying down into it the white butcher's packages of her favorite cuts of lamb, pork, and beef. But it was the fish that made her cry—the huge packages of catfish—that anchored her body, spirit all the way down to crouching on the floor and quietly sobbing. And there—head lifted up for a moment in hands—she spied it. It was standing watch, right in her line of vision, on the bottom shelf of the world-shaped liquor cabinet—a half-empty bottle of honey-dark Trinidadian rum.

"*Wifeeey*," Rodney called out, sing-songingly from the bedroom. "You bes' git *back* here, *girrr*! A bruh can't *waiiiit* all *daaay* for dat *shiiii*! Now git on *in heeere*—or I'm fuckin' you all up in *deeeere*!" He was a sick-minded child—a big, drunk and dangerous, whining, all-bashing bully baby. And there was clearly no 'no' to him. And in Shame's closed mouth, it felt as if there were no deep-back friends to easily run to, no way to tell her parents. And there were no familiar surroundings to run off, hide within—there was nothing.

P.V. sighed out the rest of her grief deeply. Reaching, she crawled forward, and then rose. Walking to the world cabinet, she squatted down again and pulled at the rum bottle. And she opened it up, strong swarthy sea and steadfastness hitting her nostrils hard from within it—that sweat of some of her peoples, hands upon hands back when to sugarcane, a sweet spoil of past oppressions. And she drank it down—all of it—all into her little self, knowing she could not hold onto it without extreme drunk to soon come. And that was the fortuitous part.

Her spirit began whispering to her that sometimes you seem so small and the area all around you so big—like the walk to the confessional with a mind full of complex sins; the wake behind the nurse in the doctor's office, as you tread in to hear what you already believe to be a dark result; and that trudge of a woman down the passageway to a bedroom against her will. It all seemed, at that instant, the very same. It was so big and looming, trapezoidal and shifting—wouldn't stay still, and was getting fuzzier with each footfall as she swaying, trod. It was surreal and blackening, and rotating off its axis, it was the longest, longest, homestead-unit walkway.

She took and tweaked Georgina and Juanita's advice, and opened the little rented condo unit into becoming an informal, potluck networking event on certain Friday nights—as Rodney was now routinely nowhere to be found from late Thursday evenings, well into Sunday afternoons. Some tasked, beginning-of-the-weekend days found her treading slowly into the farmer's market, and others, limping into it—trying to conceal in either instance the searing injuries left by Rodney between her thighs and on them, and at her arms, around her wrists. There were no shorts or mini-skirts for her on the suddenly warm days of a Texas December, or sleeves laid at ¾, biceps, or reduced to the flirty halter top strings of many moons past. The black-and-blue of layered bruising about her body, and the seemingly forever oozing ligature abrasions wrapped around her wrists prohibited her from such fashions. And altogether, each week she treaded down the rows of lush, vibrant, spilling-over stalls more of a shadow of her former flawless and bubbling self than the pain-filled and stark one before it.

And they already well knew her there at the bustling, fragrant stalls of the farmer's market; and in the ebb and flow of the out of town dairy farm, and closeby butcher shop and fish market. She was the smiling, pin-drop quiet, petite one, popping in the months prior to try out her California cooking class recipes first on Rodney, and then reluctantly, on just herself; and now perusing their offerings to try out her feeding hands on her sudden masses of others. She was always hemp shopping bags dangling on arms—ultimately filled to the heavy—the burgeoning home cook pausing to squeeze, sniff, rotate in the light, deselect, select, buy. Then, it was always the driving, mind alight, back to the little, rented condo, to follow recipes and tinker with them—and ultimately fill the faux-material unit with the fresh smells of things that were actually real.

When she was stirring four pots simultaneously, managing an active oven, and multitasking cleanup, setup, and prep, P.V.'s mind lay only on task and how best to entertain the stomachs of her upcoming guests. She gratefully escaped into the silence of active, non-thought as her fingers worked through her self-assigned, pre-party chores. And later, she felt like a mother of multiples in the snatched moments of the animated dinners, with all else fading to blur except the very visceral, intimate utility of feeding people.

The rule for P.V.'s get-togethers was that each was to bring something to share. Cooks were asked to contribute a side dish or dessert, and the foodies, any spirit-lifting accompaniment—like flowers for the table, wine, booze, or non-alcoholic beverages for the teetotalers amongst them. And with it all, she was growing in a knowledge bounding in increments about the art of being an individual, a separate person—as each assigned Friday brought more and more new hungry friends, and friends of friends, and their herstories and histories, to her door.

And because of it all, P.V. became keenly attuned to smells. She was intoxicated by the intriguing scents of people entering, with their wafts of perfumes, colognes, and unique sweat from the hours—and those of people going, infused with her foods and theirs, and the cross-aromas of fermented spirits, and good-spirited company. In those moments, too brief from evening to midnight, Rodney and his night abuses of her were in someone else's galaxy. The wine, good fare, and good company drowned him out to blank, and accordingly, the constant, wracking drumbeat of her physical, emotional, spiritual pain. It was such that for a few hours, she was actually able to feel her age, or something nearing it—until the pots, utensils, and dishes were washed. Afterwards, the sun for her sadly always brought surreally back Sunday afternoon—and Rodney—to the little rented condo unit again.

But one day, in desperation, her mother called her, stirring pots of her own, a sea breeze blowing audibly into her window. Her mother pivoted toward the panes, breathing in the wafts of sweet brine. The sounds of gusting wind blew strongly across the cell phone connection to meet P.V.'s ears. And as they did, her mother stood, wisps of stray hairs flying, wishing that her clearly hurting daughter was there. Then quietly, eyes staring out across one of the bluest of horizons, she said: "P.V., some bone a break an' heal—*quick* time. Others does tek *long*, yuh know. *Long* time. An' some...*well*. P.V.—yuh hearin' me? *Ah*? You hearin' what Mummy is *saying* to you? *Ah, P.V.*?"

They were zooming above planets, though bodies still fixed and shifting against fine, faux leather. And some were leaning forward, some back—all eyes were riveted to the physics masters onscreen. Rodney broke from the in-between-worlds journey first, swigging at an extra-large water bottle—and though substantially not fully back within the material realm, he meticulously recapped it.

"Yo, Baby—what was dat first shit you gave us? Shit was *all dat*. A mutha fucka high *for real* right now an' shit. No jokes. Got a brutha thinkin' he in the year 3055 an' shit. *Hahhhhhahaha*! Shit was mutha fuckin' *intergalactic*. Mutha fuckin' *transformational* an' shit, man!" he said hoarsely, chuckling, still transfixed by the momentum and play flashing across the medium-sized, wall-mounted, widescreen t.v. They all—his new crew of cronies—laughed, some snickering, others fully hawking out loud. He glanced about at their equally glassy eyes and faraway stares.

They were sitting in the man cave—a tiny, enclosed den, sharing a wall with the kitchen, that the owners had converted into a dark, well-appointed-looking man's entertainment room. It was a space carefully laid and furnished from floor to ceiling with faux materials—just as the rest of the little, rented condo unit—presenting as if it were, but not actually being, real. And seemingly similarly, this crew who was running with Rodney was eons away in caliber, too, from the groomsmen he had left back in California—*those* were his rocks, his road warriors, his wingmen. And *those* were enterprising young gents of distinction—highly ambitious, competitive, focused on task. He hadn't spoken to some of those guys in weeks, and he wasn't going to—chagrined that life had downspiraled so far for him economically, career-wise, and into the uncool style of depravity. He felt like one-tenth of a man at times, and at others, every bit just the toddling boy—and as a result, he believed himself first and foremost unworthy to keep his nevertheless always succeeding groomsmen's company. It seemed like everything he did these days was downsized, downgraded, scraping by, and sick to sorry—by stark contrast to the swag life he had once led. There were no manicured golf courses or slick motorcycles in this strained existence. Recalling all as if a film in playback, he winced at, then shut out, the good old days of Vegas-hopping and the attendant *ching-ching* of monetary freeness. These around him, these seven men sucking at his air, were just normal young men—struggling to exist— that he had collected in the few short weeks he had been in Texas. And yet, they were all fun amidst the funlessness, and so together, they would get lost into the eaves of the city—and in the gasses above the clouds there— at nights.

Rodney's new crew also had a harder edge, had dipped into darker activities, and seemed content with keeping things at that level in their lives. During the course of the past few moonrises, he had experienced wilder things with these than he had whilst jaunting with his groomsmen back in the day—even than on the goodbye roadtrip with his boys all the way down to Texas. But none of them seemed harder—in his own way— than Baby, a reedy, boy-faced Australian they had adopted after a brawl outside of a ghetto strip club. They nicknamed him 'Baby' because he literally looked like a child in countenance, and an overgrown teenager in body. But it was clear to Rodney, especially from that first fight, that Baby had likely *done* things—the darkest of things, things that Rodney had only really seen as a boy, over and over and over again and not spoken of, in his forgotten side of L.A.

Baby was the only one completely glowing in the flashing, flatscreen kaleidoscope against semi-darkness. He laughed softly in response to Rodney's query without speaking, a mysterious and beckoning characteristic of his demeanor. It was a breathy, knowing, earthy chuckle of a young man who perhaps thought it best—given his past and/or present—to forever hold his tongue, offer up nothing, yield to everything.

"Ah-*ight*, Baby," Rodney remarked, grinning.

From deep in the den quasi-blackness, in the outskirts of the t.v. glow, one of the crew shot forth a suggestion. "Mm-*hm*! An' one a dese days, Baby gon' have ta answer *dat* question, an' da one we all *really* wanna know—which is exactly how many mutha fuckas you done *kilt*, man? An' *why*, for example, probably ain' no mutha fuckas lef' to tell the tale after they done got into a fist-fight wit' you, man? Well—except for dat one brutha we know 'bout. Dat brutha Rodney done saved—*hahahahaha*!" They all in the room snickered in response, glancing at each other knowingly—except for one.

"See now, *dere* you go," Rodney agreed, smiling slightly, "I *must* be a *savior*, right? 'Cause *dat* mutha fucka was goin' *down* ta Baby over dere, an' *hard*—*wa'n't* he? Thank you, dawg. Dat's a *serious*, mutha fuckin' *legitimate-ass* question." The entire detail was chuckling, eyes sidelong at the only man who wasn't, as they tossed back longneck beers, and grasped at fistfuls of naked tortilla chips. Rodney's second-hand man cleared his throat, and tossed forward an inquiry of his own from the back row of chairs.

"Yo, *Rod*, speaking a questions—lemme ask *you* one. Seriously, bruh—how is you married an' runnin' so *hard* wit' us, dawg? I mean, this Texas—I ain' never run wit' no married dude before, yo. I mean...*shiiit*—we be runnin' all night, all mornin'—you know that. I mean, look at all the shit we be gittin' up to an' into, man! Yeah—most a us got a honey tucked away somewhere, you know, but that's just for insurance an' economics an' shit. You know, someone who could say you was there, e'en when you wasn't—an' who can feed yo' ass an' float you a couple dollas when you need it. That kinda thang. But I mean...we ain't, you know, *tied down* to no one or nuthin' like *that*. *Shiiit*—most a us divorced or ain' e'en been married yet. It's just easier dat way. Nobody aroun' to mutha fuckin' *nag* you, or need nuthin' *from* you, or nuthin' like *that*. I mean, some a us got kids here an' there—but that's *another* mutha fuckin' story. They hard here on that kinda shit, anyway—so e'erybody know you *do* have to pay yo' muh fuckin' child support up in the T-X—but, dat don't mean you got to be *married* or really *deal* wit' yo' baby mama or nuthin' like *that*. So, I mean, dawg—*hard* as we run—*why is you married?* What's the mutha fuckin' *point?*" The room was struck silent, the rest waiting to hear whether Rodney would take the question as a challenge, or as a chance to reveal more about himself. They all secretly salivated for his marital insider tips, if he had any to offer.

"Uh-*huh. Anyway.* Remember who house you in an' mind yo' mutha fuckin' business, man," Rodney replied gruffly, chugging at a different local beer—a newly discovered by P.V., fave of his—that she had neatly stocked the fridge with for him. "But for da record—I married a island girl, who didn' know *shit* about men before I married her, an' who does what I *tell* her to. Hope dat helps y'all ladies."

It was quiet for a minute, and then another, grinning, spoke up. "Uhhh—I 'on't know 'bout dat, bruh. *I* dated a island girl who was kinda naïve an' stuff, *too*. But when she found out a young brutha was *cheatin'* on her, she looked me dead up in da eyes an' broke *ev'ry mutha fuckin' glass* in a young bruh's house. An' *den* her fine, fat, green-card-havin' *ass* jus' *lef' out* like *'peace out'*—an' a young bruh was lef' wit' nothin' but empty plates, an' a crib-full a memories, an' enough shards ta fuck up a whole gang a mutha fuckas or create one mutha fuckin' crazy-ass collage an' shit. So—I 'on't *know*, man. I 'on't *know*." The crew descended into laughter at his winking account—all except for Rodney—some coughing at the tail of their mirth from too many hours spent playing at chemicals.

"*Anyway*," Rodney barked.

"*Anyway, Cali*," yet another of the crew, emboldened, piped up at Rodney, as the one sucked down the remnants of his third longneck. "Uh, changin' the subject to da one we watchin' at hand? Uh—y'all can't win all da rings, dawg—we for *real* an' we comin' for ours, an' that ain't no *lie*. So, uh, L.A.—bettah ha' my money ready." The most of the detail uttered 'ooing' noises in a show of support, packaged with bolstering rounds of *'right-right?'*

Rodney snickered at them all, throwing back another dose of his specially-bought brew. "Y'all fans down here a trip an' a half. I *gi'* you dat—you git props for passion an' shit. But it ain't y'all dudes' year—an' it ain' *never* gon' be. Could be, but y'all just don't *got* it. Ain' hungry enough or afraid a success or some shit like dat. I may be *down* here, but y'all right about one thing—I ain' no *convert.* I be rootin' for my *homedawgs*—uh, *both* a dem. But as to da one *you* speakin' of, what can I say? It's called a *proven track record* a mutha fuckin' *success*—dat comes from bein' mutha fuckin' *relentless.* It's called bein' a gang a *hungry* mutha fuckas—ready for da win— each an' e'ery mutha fuckin' time."

"*Psssht*—you think it ain't gon' happen? Oh, it *gon'* happen," the one insisted, his voice raising slightly. "E'erythang *bigger*—an' *bettah*—in da *Big D*, yo. An' we got da *frills* an' da *skills* ta make shit *happen. Shiit.* An' jus' 'cause you *said* dat, we should take a rollin' bet—raisin' up double e'ery year 'till it *do* happen."

Rodney laughed out loud, choking and coughing slightly after another chug of his beer. "You slick mutha fuckin' hustlah—now who gon' take a bet like *dat*—let alone on *y'all* team? *Hahahahaha*—go 'head wit' all dat, *hahaha.* Like I *said*, dey ain' *never* gon' wear no rings. An' if dey *do*—an' dat's a big mutha fuckin' *'if'*—I'm a be long *gone* from Texas 'fore dat. *Shiit.*" And for a moment, when Rodney said it, he felt re-tethered to his gold bar, glorious past in California. But then the contents of the room jolted him back to a set of stark facts—waking him up to the reality that he had slid so far, perhaps too far, from home.

"*Gone? Gone? Shiit.* Now, where is you *goin'*, playa?"

"Anyway," Rodney grunted. "But *yo*—I toss you a *bone*, lil' dawg. A brutha *do* like your cheerleaders, though—*for real.*"

They all murmured heartily in agreement, snickering and stretching out to clink bottles with each other. "Yo, best in da league—*for real*," one of them added. "An' uh…if dem cheerleaders turn up missin', yo—dey at my house. An' uh…don't worry about it—don't worry about it. Dey *will* be *well* taken care of." He raised his lips into a mischievous grin, and patted his crotch. A chorus of laughter sprang up from the group, and nearby hands reached out to reward him with a congratulatory slap for his fitting contribution.

"*Yo, yo, Rod*—you got any ginger ale, man?" the one who hadn't laughed earlier, one called Pussy, interrupted weakly. A barely 20, squat young man with a long, wide, and somewhat recent keloid scar running diagonally across his forehead, he was leaning eyes-shut forward, rubbing his stomach. Tears of sweat were beginning to form at his temples and fall, streaming, down his dark, t.v.-glow-blue-lit cheeks. He had been profoundly nauseous ever since 7 o'clock that morning, immediately after wolfing down breakfast at the infamous café . He knew—mind, spirit, tapping at him—that it wasn't the food that had done him in so queasy. He trusted that place. They'd never let him or his belly down. Besides, two of the guys that he'd partied wild with, well into the new day, had eaten the very same—migas with ample salsa, orange juice, coffee—and had left whistling and laughing into the fully risen sun. He knew and was afraid of what it was and he wanted to stamp it out—jam at it with a boot and be done with it—that thing he shaking, believed it to be. But he knew he could not—that it was real, and that it would hauling, take him. He rose to his feet, an unsteady, broken down crewman.

"*Damn*, man," Rodney remarked, looking up at Pussy's dour countenance sideways, pinching up a large cross-section of the thin and sprawling tortilla chips as he did so. "You really *is* sick. Well *go on* den, Typhoid Mary."

"Naw, man—I just need some ginger ale. Den I'll be straight." The entire crew was staring up at Pussy as he spoke, taking in his perspiration, tremble, and sway. He looked as if he'd witnessed a terror in his eyes—something was clearly, profoundly wrong.

"Well, look in the fridge, den," Rodney offered casually. "Wifey always got a big batch a her homemade ginger beer up in dere. That shit'll clean yo' mutha fuckin' *clock*, though—*for real.*"

"Thanks, man," Pussy breathed, relieved—but he turned the other way out of the room first, tripping in his haste to make it in time to the nearby guest bathroom. They all laughed at him, some of them loudly making retching noises in his wake.

As they came down, one of them asked, "Seriously, though—you a lucky ass man, Rod. Homegirl be throwin' down like *dat* in da kitchen? Whippin' up *beverages* an' shit, too? *Dang*—I needs to git me a island girl, *too*, man. *For real.*"

"I'm tryin' ta *tell* ya," Rodney replied coolly, taking a healthy swig of his unique beer. "Only way ta go for *me*. An' I was serious when I said dat Trinidadian ginger beer a hers ain' no fuckin' joke—dat shit so rowdy, I swear one night it hopped outta da pitcher an' started hustlin' me for change, an' shit." The crew laughed, booming out again, slapping knees and holding stomachs, and settling back cozy into the lush, faux leather couch and chairs. A couple of them put their cowboy- and workman's-booted feet up on the massive, faux mahogany wood-and-glass coffee table.

"Yeah—but dat ain't gonna help Pussy none," yet another piped up, jerking his head and slapping a handful of beer nuts back.

Baby instantly, but casually, rose to his feet—a lean, puerile-faced young man of medium height, cleanly propelling upward. A longneck in one hand, he wiped his mouth meticulously on the cuff of his leather jacket sleeve. Then, reaching into the inside pocket of his jacket for something with the other, he strode purposefully—hard on cowboy-boot heels—out of the room. And a few moments later, with a creak, he turned in the direction of the guest bathroom.

"I swear sometimes Baby a chemist on the run an' shit," Rodney's number one man offered, chuckling.

"Right? Shit—runaway chemist wit' da keys to da mutha fuckin' strip club all-stars, in e'erybody's house he know, an' shit," Rodney finished gleefully, to a round of laughter from his crew.

"Right-right?" his number one agreed. "Sometimes I be wakin' up in my bed after one a Baby's friends' parties an' shit an' be like, '*yo*—did I jus' *dream* all that shit?'" The crew hooted and chortled, murmuring their own attestations to each other husky and low across the air.

"Y'all though-y'all though—like I was sayin' before, though—Pussy ain't sick from nuthin' you can heal," the first speaker interjected. "He sick 'cause he bumped into Miss Vernetta at dat damn lil' restaurant café we like on da East side an' shit. It's 'cause she *touched* him an' shit. *Told* him to stay away from dat place—*knew* he'd mess aroun' an' git himself got."

"What?!" Rodney uttered, incredulous—pitch raised, glancing back at the speaker in the semi-darkness. "What's dat got ta do wit' anything?"

Vernetta and the Reverend were a regionally well-known, husband-and-wife preaching and urban missionary team, that operated a small, Baptist-offshoot, non-denominational church tucked neatly into East Dallas. Affectionately and deferentially referred to by the locals as 'Miss Vernetta' and 'Rev.', they made it a determined point to visit local bars, clubs, and late night restaurants—as well as pancake houses, and other eateries that operated until the wee hours, or opened their doors early for breakfast. Their standard operating procedure when inside each proprietorship was to pass out their church business cards, inviting certain recipients to Sunday worship and healing services, but they rarely visited establishments as a couple—they typically canvassed for souls solo. Rodney had encountered them—together—whilst walking with P.V., on a leisurely stroll past the very same East Dallas café and restaurant, during his first few days in Texas. Rev. had extended a card to him, but Vernetta oddly just glared at him from Rev.'s side. Rodney, immediately irritated, waived the card away, yet instructed P.V. to take it from Rev.—and never thought for a moment to retrieve it from her later.

"Mm-*hm*—dat woman's got da *touch*! Dey say if she lay hands on you—you gon' git *saved*—whetha ya *wants to* or *not*," the one continued, standing to stretch, gesturing with his beer bottle as he spoke. "*Shii*—happened to a ol' runnin' dawg a mine, Randy—when I was out wit' him after a nice, looong-ass night."

Rodney twisted his body up to look at the one, and narrowing his eyes, peered at him intently. "Well—go on, dawg. I mean, if you gon' *tell* a ghost story, then mutha fuckin' *tell* it. Pausin' an' shit like dis live theater. Go *on*." The crew laughed, shaking their heads and nudging each other as they did so. Baby, quick-striding, returned from the direction of the bathroom and Pussy—minus the beer that was in his hand and the company of the same, and forcefully tucking an empty plastic baggie back into his inner jacket pocket. Some eyed him curiously in the glow, quiet but eager to know what had been occurring around the corner.

The one regarded him too, but continued, inadvertently shrugging and shaking his head. "Ah-*ight*. After you *told*, you *sold*, dawg. So here it is, Rodney, my brutha. It was one a dem nights when me an' Randy an' some other cats was runnin' like all a us, you know—drinkin' hard, smokin' hard, rollin' hard, fuckin' hard—all night, into da nex' day. Matta fact, Randy said dat night it was da hardest he'd ever rode in his muh fuckin' existence an' shit. He actually said dat when da sun rose, he was ten times higher dan *dat* muh fucka." The crew chortled healthily in a burst, some thrown back in their chairs by the twin brute forces of glee and truth.

"*Right?* I see y'feelin' me," the one remarked, profoundly pleased by their response. "*Hahahahaha!* So, *anyways*, after we had parted ways dat mornin', Randy had went by his ex-girlfriend house an' shit—an' though he looked all fucked up an' shit, she took him in. Now, *why* bitches be takin' us in, lookin' like we been up in eight million pussies an' shit, I 'on't understan', but oh *well*—an' bless dey simple asses. Y'all know dem chicks always be messed up in shit dey shouldn't be, 'cause a us, an' it don't never help none a dem, no how. But a course, like bruh over here was sayin', we know we all depen' on dey simple asses for a variety a thangs, so we jus' got ta do what we got ta do an' move on an' not feel sorry for what we be doin' to dey lives an' shit. Jus' had ta preach dat. *Anyway*, *dat* chick said he had to be out well before noon, 'cause her man liked ta come over den, so a brutha had ta leave. So Randy decided he was jus' gon' git breakfas' at all our muh fuckin' *favorite* spot—same one all a us like to hit up after a nice night, all da way across town, on da Eas' Side. Now, a brutha had gone home, but couldn't sleep—y'all know how it is—so I had decided to jus' haul on over dere den, an' me an' Randy ended up showin' up right aroun' da same time. So, anyway, da food came, an' we was jus' cuttin' up an' talkin' stories about da night—an' den who should walk up ta our table from somewhere up in dere, but Rev.'s wife, Miss Vernetta. I mean, all dressed up like Sunday an' shit, wit' dem beautiful tits an' dat tight, juicy ass—*whooo*. Y'all *know* Miss Vernetta fine," he paused, panting and sweating, hands clenched in ecstasy, as all but Baby—who had not yet encountered Vernetta or her husband—eagerly murmured their agreement.

"*Right?*" the one proceeded. "Jus' a looking like dat cartoon bunny's wife back in day—wha's her name ag'in?"

One of the crew yelled out from the darkness, "Rabbit!"

"Right—*right*! Y'all *know* dat chick be straight up lookin' like a mutha fuckin' black J. Rabb an' shit—*ooh*!" The most of them in the room nodded, murmuring in tandem their attestations.

"*Right?*" the speaker launched on excitedly. "So, anyway, like e'erybody, we had already heard dat Miss V. got da Touch an' shit—dat she tap you, an' yo' ass be turnin' over to da Lord—*e'erybody* heard dat one. So, Randy was already lookin' nervous, when she was walkin' up ta us, you know? An' *shiii*—I was buggin' too…but dat was 'cause da problem is dat Miss Vernetta a pretty assed woman an' shit—an' since I was still high as a muh fuckin' kite an' shit, I was fuckin' scared a what muh fuckin' crazy-assed, inappropriate shit I might slip up an' say ta her ass." The crew all snickered— knowing, cutting sounds cycling all throughout the open space.

"*Right-right!* Ag'in—I see y'all still feelin' me. So, anyway, needless ta say, two bruthas was all cringin' *way* back into da booth. *Shiit*—we both had forkfuls a some a da best migas I ever tasted in my muh fuckin' life— dat kitchen was *kickin' it* dat mornin'—an' den *she* walk up. I couldn' even put da mutha fuckin' fork down an' shit—it was like, halfway to my mouth, but I was *mesmerized* an' shit. An' den somethin' said, 'bite her'." The detail laughed out in unison, heads bowing and shaking with the gravity of both the humor and the inappropriateness. "I'm serious, y'all," he urged, smiling. "a) I was high dat night, b) I was also drunk—y'all know how we do—an', c) y'all *know* I ain't mutha fuckin' right," he tapped the temple of his forehead with a forefinger, as regards the latter, for effect, grinning widely.

"So anyway," the one marched on, smile rapidly disappearing from his face, "Miss Vernetta taps Randy on da shoulder, an' looks dead into his mutha fuckin' eyes—her just a grinnin', an' him just a grimacin' an' shit. So den she started sayin' 'good mornin' an' stuff like dat—an' all I could hear out Randy' mouth was 'yes ma'am, no ma'am—ma'am?' An' *den* she looked at his forkful a migas—he still hadn't even put *his* fork down an' shit—an' said how dere's dis church right around da corner an' dat dey Ladies Auxiliary Guild would fix him up some eats jus' right—an' dat one a dem was gon' be his wife. Straight up. I mean, da chick was *predictin'* an' shit! Muh fuckin' *prophetess* action an' shit! *Yo.* An' *den* she jus' *smiled* at him. *Den* she turned her head an' looked at *me*—*dead* up in da eyes, *too*—but...she didn't say shit *to* me, or *touch* me, or *nuthin'*. An' den...she lef' out."

The room was eerily silent—the only sounds those of the ebb and flow of the play-by-play of the basketball game, emanating from the beaming t.v.

"*So?*" Rodney said crisply, unaffected, popping down a handful of beer nuts. "I mean, I think me an' Wifey bumped into da two a dem once—an' I mean, if it *was* her, *yeah* she fine. So? So—a sexy-ass reverend's wife interrupted yo' asses at breakfast, right after y'all was rollin' an' ballin', an' said yo' frien' should date some chick at her an' her husband's round-da-way church. *And?*"

"Patience, my brutha—*patience*. Da 'and' is—*and*, nex' thang I know, muh fuckin' seven weeks later, no joke, here come Randy callin' me on da cell when I was jus' gittin' up from gittin' my yum-yum on. You know how we all do—I had to say 'excuse me, Miss' quite a few times 'fore I could really talk, *hahahahaha*. An' *believe* a a bruh was so high off so much jacked up shit dat earlier, he was outside, buck nekked an' moon-howlin' at one point an' shit. *Anyway*, dere was all dis noise in da backgroun', so I asked dude where he was at. An' he said dat he was at a fish fry at his church, dat he had jus' got *saved*, dat he had *met a girl* dere, an' dat she was helpin' him ta *stay* saved. *Den* he said I shouldn' call him 'Randy' no mo', dat dat was jus' his middle name, an' dat now he goin' by his firs' name— 'Isaiah', an' shit. *Den* he said he was callin' me 'cause he jus' know *I* needed ta be saved—dat very day. *Den*, he was sayin' how he wanted ta come ta my house, ta talk 'bout bein' born ag'in, an' how I *needs* ta be born ag'in…An' I was like, 'hold up, hold up, hold up, Randy—*Isaiah*. I mean, you need *help* a somethin'? What da *fuck* dey put in dat muh fuckin' fish fry batter an' shit, hah? I mean, what da *fuck*?'" The crew all laughed—mostly a bit uneasily—into the deepening semi-darkness, highly appreciative of the one speaking their own knee-jerk, natural thoughts. But their skins were secretly crawling at the results of his tale.

"Ah-*iight*?" the one responded, gesturing with his beer. "Now y'all *well* know after *dat*, dat I didn' want dat mutha fucka all up in my *house*— besides, it was an inconvenient-ass time an' shit. But, anyway—dat's my fuckin' story, yo. *Truth.* So, Miss V. ain' no joke—she *fine*, but if she *git* you, you *gone* from dese here pleasures—I *guarantee*. An' by da way, Baby—now *yo'* crazy ass know dis shit. So, if yo' ass be up in dere an' some muh fuckin' Sunday-dressed, beautiful-assed, black doll approach yo' table—I know dis gon' sound wild, 'cause I know yo' ass a equal opportunity mutha fucka an' shit—but fo' yo' own muh fuckin' sake an' livelihood, try ta look da mutha fuck away, y'heard? An' it gon' hurt you—'cause you gon' wanna—but don' let dat hot-ass chick touch you, dawg. She sexy, but she holy—serious, convertin'-yo'-ass holy—remember dat shit, 'cause she gon' fuck wit' yo' head behin' all dat, an' den yo' wayward ass gon' end up in *somebody* church, an' wonder how da mutha fuck you got dere, an' shit. On da real, I think dat's *exactly* what dat chick designed ta do. An' don' be thinkin' you big, an' can wit'stan' her muh fuckin' holy-ass tap, jus' 'cause you done probably kilt 95 mutha fuckas across the earth dat we don' know about an' shit. Matta fact, *I* say, since you don't know what she look like yet an' shit, don't let *none* a dem fine, churchy-assed chicks bounce up an' touch you like dat—all on account a dat might actually be Miss Vernetta. 'Cause if it *is* her, on *yo'* ass gon' belong to da Spirit in like, seven mutha fuckin' days an' shit—an' den you gon' be callin' an' naggin' another playa 'bout it, talkin' 'bout how you been saved, an' how dey need ta be saved—an' all from some mutha fuckin' wherever-y'all-go-down-in-Australia-ta-git-yo'-church-an'-eat-on-at-da-same-muh-fuckin'-time, an' shit. I mean—'cause a her, I cain' even git my fuckin' fried fish on an' shit now. Scared if I eat dat shit, I might git converted-by-mutha-fuckin'-proxy an' shit. Y'all don' know what a brutha be *dealin'* wit' sometimes over dat shit—'specially at lunchtime. *Shiit. Told.*"

The crew, which had been chuckling throughout, erupted into bouts of laughter—Baby the hardest and heartiest, shaking his head incredulously and still chortling, as he tipped back a beer. Another of the crew yelled out into the fray, "*Shoooooot*—you go tell Miss V. dat I don' *want* the Holy Ghos' yet—'cause I got some nasty *shit* lef' ta *dooo*! Oh—an' tell her, fine or no fine, I cain't be *takin'* on no *stress* from no *chick* like dat when I'm trying' ta git my *eats* on—y'all know a brutha ride hard an' shit! I needs my muh fuckin' *calories*!" They all descended into guffaws again, acknowledging his sentiments in their side commentaries. "*Naw*—y'all don't understand," he continued, smirking amidst their laughter, "Ruin a brutha good *digestion* an' shit—who do dat, man? Who *do* dat?"

Another of the crew offered, "*Shoo*—call *me* up from a muh fuckin' fish fry talkin' 'bout 'I found-t da Lawd an' you should too' an' shit! *Uh*-uh! I'm wit' bruh man over dere—den I'll jus' muh fuckin' stay out da sea wit' my dietary consumptions an' shit. No water residents—I say, no *water residents* for a brutha! *Shiiit.* I *luh* rollin' an' fuckin'—so I cain't takes no *chances*! Hahahahaha. Besides, y'all know *me*—I be *90* an' *still* reaching fo' dat tin a sin. So I hope da Ghost don' be tellin' Miss V. where ta come find *my* breakfast-lovin' ass!"

Rodney shook his head, smirking amidst the new round of chortles, swigging again at the fizzy, stinging remnants of yet another of his lovingly-bought beers. "Y'all straight up crazy," he muttered.

The original speaker piped up again, adamant. "Ain' no crazy *to* it dawg. You jus' ain' been aroun' long enough, Cali. All a us from da D know da deal. *Yo*—but here's da truly creepy thang, though, dawg—dey say dat Rev. touch different. Dat if Miss Vernetta touch you, you gon' git saved—but if *Rev.* touch you, you gon' git saved one way or da other."

"What?!" Rodney queried, irritated—voice pitched up high, struck serious all of a sudden. "What's *dat* supposed ta mean?"

"*Dat* supposed ta mean if you ain't right an' Miss Vernetta touch you, you gon' be *saved* by da Spirit. If you walkin' wrong an' Rev. touch you, you might actually *meet* da Spirit, my brutha." The one raised his eyebrows for effect, as he took a sip of, similar to most in the room, his nth beer. The room fell human-quiet again for a moment, and then others slowly, earnestly, began to chime in their support of his contentions, murmuring, '*word*' and '*I heard that too*'.

"Man—*shut* up," Rodney uttered forcefully to the one—and trying to silence the all—brow knit, face frowning, turning head and torso back to the screen. Balancing his elbows on his knees, he reached out again, to grab their communal, plastic baggie from its resting place at the edge of the coffee table. It was a pristinely clear, large freezer bag full of various, brightly-hued chemical goodies—a hodge-podge of pills and patches that Baby had, per their usual game-night-any-night routine, brought. "You don't know *shit*," he concluded roughly, glaring swiftly, reproachfully, back at the speaker over a shoulder. And then he cocked his head well back—in line with the ceiling—and sprinkled a fistful of pills, like multi-colored candies, into his nevertheless inexplicably quivering, empty mouth.

That Texas morning, P.V.'s little body was still drugged down as if with morphine, by the excessive amount of rum she had consumed the agonizing night before. In vain, she had tried to once again black out, mentally escape, Rodney's soulless and shoving, sexual aggression. It was then—still drawn down by the anesthetic undertow—that she again dreamt of Nani.

Nani was stray hairs flying in the ocean wind all about her, long braid now jet black and shiny—not a grey in natural sight, from peaked crown to tip. Her face and body too, had regressed to the tight, lighter brown and glistening of her youth. The latter had additionally returned to the perfect litheness that well preceded the middle-thickness occasioned by her series of childbirths. And she was princess-perfectly balanced on tiny, brown feet that were wrapped in sparkling, gold sandals, like an everyday ballerina. P.V. instantly realized from deep within her own spirit, and her remembrance of Nani's wedding photos, that Nani was presenting just as she had before she was married off: she was clearly in her late teens again, and utterly breathtaking.

And Nani was swathed in the traditional rich, bright red silk, embroidered at its edges with patterns hewn of sparkling, metallic gold thread. All of the free corners of the garment were sweeping up at intervals like her wisps, in the strong, gusting air. She was standing on a beach unrecognizable to P.V., the sun bouncing at play behind her on big and lovely, green-blue waters. Waves began to curl up and rush quick in to the portion of sand just beyond her heels. And P.V. could hear the muffled sounds of people laughing and calling out to each other in the background, although the people themselves were not in view. Nani smoothed a few hairs back from her face errantly, as young women sometimes do, revealing intricate patterns inked onto the skin of both hands. A layer of shiny gold bangles clinked musically, soothingly, with her motion, like hanging garden chimes. She was regarding P.V. intently and smiling, dark eyes misty and sparkling, and radiating emotion.

"Nani! Nani!" P.V. called out to her, above the fray. "What is this? What is this place?"

Nani pointed and inclined her head at P.V.—several times—uttering the same reply without sound, the big water funneling high behind her intermittently as she did so. Each time, the smoothly arcing, massive body immediately subsided, into a sweet, small-waving calm. P.V. discerned the first part of the word Nani kept mouthing, but repeatedly lost whatever was attached to it. She could glean only, "Oce-an…, Oce-an…", which, from the continued motion of Nani's lips, trailed off into something at least two beats more.

Nani suddenly turned her head to an area on the sand just beyond her gold-sandaled feet. A clear wine glass, with a large, rounded body, was standing, without accompaniment, on what appeared to be a plank of dark wood. The vessel was full almost to its brim with a deeply red, swirling wine—the liquid tipping to and fro in the glass, catching the white reflection of the sun, although no one was holding it. From a distance, the wine actually appeared to be thin, non-oxidized blood. Thick black clouds sprang ballooning out from nowhere over the glass and blanketed around the dark plank, and instantaneously, the glass tipped—its contents spilling out onto the plank, creating a creeping puddle on its surface. And all around it arose a brighter red, viscous liquid—a pool of spreading, exposed human blood. Then the two—the wine and the blood—they intermingled.

Nani looked sharply up at P.V., shaking her head in disbelief. Then her lids downcast once more, to the dark and dripping plank. She pointed at the crawling red mess, which began to swirl dangerously near her glinting sandals, and then gazing up at P.V., pointed again at the swimming liquids.

As she did so, all of it dried up into itself. And, together with the wine glass and the dark plank, everything there summarily vanished.

Stunned, breath almost sucked from her body, P.V. tried to walk toward Nani, hands outstretched, with the intent to touch her. But the sands began to retract *en masse* underneath her bare feet, as if a conveyer belt retreading her back. And a frontal gale-force wind kicked up and pushed at her from the head, torso, knees—insistently, and away from, the scene.

P.V. awoke with a start. A large, involuntary contraction instantly flexed her entire body, the impact of it jolting her out of the narrow sliver of bed space reserved for her, and onto the floor. The vibration of the thud roused Rodney from his deep-sleeping, noiseless stupor. Naked, he lazily propped himself up on one elbow, staring blankly down at P.V. from high upon the black and satiny, polyester bed sheets. Somehow, a part of his newly lanky body seemingly occupied every quadrant of the queen-sized domain.

"*Dang*, girl," he remarked casually, eyeing up P.V.'s nude body. She had curled, wincing, up into a partial fetal position on the floor. Her cold flesh was covered in puckering goose-pimples, still smarting in darts all about it from the heavy fall. "What's up, yo? *Daaang.* I ain't even *touched* you yet, an' you *already* black an' blue."

P.V. stared back at him, feeling as if a wild animal trapped, being observed as prey, nervous as to what move the predator might next make. A thought occurred to her as she lay there, startled and paining, that even a friend, a roommate, a stranger would have leapt over and made an attempt to save, help her. And just then, as the sun pushed blindingly in from the fully open, metal venetian blinds, she smelt sandalwood—Nani's favorite scent—everywhere in the tiny bedroom air. Rodney yawned and shifted— stretching—in the creaking bed, ultimately folding his torso up to sitting.

He sat smirking at P.V., letting the seconds roll in the still, a few frightening pulses more. Then he leaned a little forward, and opened his twisting mouth. "Come here, girl," he said.

Had she been expecting company, she would have concealed them. But hearing her groaning, crying uncontrollably from outside the atypically half-open condo unit door, Georgina and Juanita rushed in—only to find P.V. in a heap on the floor in front of the kitchen sink, loosely clutching her smartphone in one hand. And they could hear the sing-song of her mother's voice flying frantically out from the cell phone, echoing all around it, screaming, wailing as her child was wailing too.

"*P.V.? P.V.? Oh my gohd…oh my gohd*…child, *tell* me—*tell* Mummy, nuh! *Tell me*—what's *wrong?* Who hurtin' you? Who *hurtin'* you? *Oh gohd…oh my gohd*…is dat *mahn*…is dat *mahn*! I *know* it—I *know* it! *Oh gohd…oh my gohd.* Sanjay! Sanjay!! Come *help* me, nuh!! *Oh my gohd*…Sanjay—dat *mahn*—is dat *mahn*…he killin' up P.V.! He *killin'* she! *Oh gohd…oh my gohd*…P.V.? P.V.? *Oh my gohd*…"

And P.V. was slumped and rocking, a crumpled skin within the short-sleeved baby doll dress that bared her arms and legs. Juanita and Georgina exchanged glances as they neared her. They were four eyes seeing for the first time the deep, black-blue bruising on her tan forearms, and the series of abrasions in the entire skin around both wrists—the latter appeared as if she had been tied or cuffed by them, and then had further struggled against the restraints on them for unyielding periods of time. Their eyes traveled down, too, to the multiple purple-blue bruises on her exposed upper thighs, the inner of one, the outer of another—visible, screaming their pain, plain in the light of the Texas day.

Georgina gently plucked the cell phone from P.V.'s limp, half-open fist, and spoke to P.V.'s mother, promising to call her back with a full report, once they could manage the situation. Then the two together, Georgina and Juanita, helped P.V.—half-walking, doubled over cramping and sobbing—to the couch. And in a joint hug, they held her, rocking her like a wee one. It was in that new, little circle of comfort and compassion, that she Told them, tears streaming from her eyes like torrential rains down windows.

They stayed with P.V. that night—with the knowledge that Rodney would not likely return until late into the next day—and called their husbands in those hushed hours to let them know that everything was not the same with everybody. She told them that she thought she had been hemorrhaging blood, too—leaking from everywhere that there was no daylight—and oozing from other wounds that she equally could not bear to squat and hold a hand mirror to, shocked, see. Alarmed by the amount of blood that she had in fact output in front of them, they begged her to go to the emergency room—but profoundly embarrassed, she over and over again refused, compromising only to set an appointment with an ob/gyn instead. And reluctantly, they took that unreasonable risk to honor her request, and sat with her while she called one. Then they fed her, sang to her, dressed her in her pajamas, and smoothed her head as she entered into the darkened, sweet realm of sleep. And then when she had dropped off into the visiting arms of Morpheus, they exchanged glances once more, and picking up her smartphone, they click-dialed and Told her mother.

The room walls were washed in pale pink, and the almost similarly-hued, expansive floor was laid in deliberately worn-looking slats of natural oak laminate. In the middle of the room, amongst the light grey hospital-grade cabinetry, sink, and chairs, were P.V. and the examination table. And she felt alone as she lay there flat on her back, knees high on that strange bed, hospital-gowned with a sheet across her upturned lap. Georgina and Juanita had insisted on accompanying her, but Fear and Shame—the twin isolators—had tricked her into resisting their support. So there she was, praying on the inside, hands protectively on her stomach, eyes cast down on the crown of the ob/gyn's head. Her plump cheeks were long, with a face set in the anxious, the blood seemingly all drawn out from within it. She was heart in throat, soul in feet, waiting for all of her festering secrets to be revealed.

The doctor actually seemed to be much younger than she—a decidedly fresh-faced, slim-boned Indian woman, sporting a black and shiny, brush-like at the ends, ultra short ponytail. And she was assisted by the middle-aged blonde nurse with eyes full of surprise and empathy, who had originally ushered P.V. into the room.

P.V. winced and kicked throughout the entirety of the pelvic exam and pap smear, thrashing frequently amidst the waves of a searing, all-below pain. Her knees buckled in toward each other several times, involuntarily jolting out of the stirrups, and she half-sat up twice, bleating and in tears like a tortured baby lamb.

"*Sorry*, honey—*so, so*, sorry, honey. I'm *so* sorry," the doctor said quietly, soothingly, in an ambling Texas accent cut with something almost musical. "Awl-*most* duhn, honey. You jes hang in there f'r me if y'can. Jes one more—I promise!" And indeed, although it had seemed an eternity, the ob/gyn concluded her examination quickly, glancing up meaningfully at the nurse as she shut off her surgical lamp and ripped off her gloves. And then they left her for a moment, swiftly and soundlessly, the air of all things heavy about them.

A shuddering P.V. struggled to pull on her clothes, feeling every ache throughout her body from Rodney's bedroom vitriol, and every blazing cut of flesh between her legs from the same. She sat still, almost to the breath, in one of the guest chairs, waiting for the ob/gyn to return.

The doctor walked in and pulled a swivel chair in front of P.V., feet planted on the floor and apart like a winded athlete, torso leaning slightly toward her. She held a set of local assistance brochures in her long, light brown hands. "Um…Mrs..." she began.

"Um, j-just 'P.V.'," P.V. stammered, closing her jacket about her neck in one tiny, quivering fist.

The doctor nodded, thin face set like cement. She looked across into P.V.'s eyes—at one then the other, and back and again, searching for the revelation. And then she told her what she had found—how unspeakably torn P.V. was in that place between her legs—noting too, the deep purple-blue bruising on her thighs, legs, arms, and the abrasions forming bracelets of drying, raw flesh around her wrists. Then she paused, area outreach pamphlets still in hand, eyes inquiring before her mouth. So, P.V. answered her tacit query and Told her, too. She Told her all of it—all about the mind-, spirit-, body-degrading night after violent night with Rodney, about the sick each and everything. A straight wall of tears raced down from her eyes, coating her face, as hiccoughing, in detail she recounted It. But, then she didn't wish to speak of It anymore—or be spoken unto about It. And thus, the pamphlets in the ob/gyn's hands were more speedily transferred to hers, and gingerly, she rose—as if profoundly elderly in bearing—body wracked with pain and shaking. And hobbling, she took the stock-photoed brochures, with all of their words and contact numbers and websites, together with the each and every one of her manifest brokennesses, back to home—back to the little, rented, fear-filled, faux home.

The empty bar and almost vacant, breezy restaurant wrapped around it were outfitted in all that was clean lines contemporary. A lipstick orchid pink, futuristic dark turquoise, and crisp, neon lime furtively—coolly—intermingled at the bar's backlighting and the restaurant's ceiling spotlights. Together with the turquoise, metallic-glinting, granite bar top, those portions of the space winked with all that was intriguing about clubs and lounges at night. But they weren't sufficient. P.V.'s soul was already elsewhere, instantly, curiously wishing back not just for California, but for another escape entirely.

Something had been stirring in her earlier, as she limped down the hardtop aisles of the farmer's market, bouncing up beets, inhaling and squeezing at tomatoes, and sifting like a treasure-collector through for the best from the cornucopia of pecans. It was at first simply a strong longing for an elsewhere, and then softening, it became a quiet realization that there actually *was* a life for her waiting somewhere in the world—a place to its very core better for her. And that place, her spirit began to tell her, held for her a sweet-aired blissful existence, in part because it would be completely free from the overlapping wounds of physical and psychological, marital pain. But before she could tap into her awakening self for the where that almost mythical, easier-for-her destination was, her viridescent ballerina flats had tapping, led her—arms overwhelmed with her organic grocery bags and searing at their bruised parts—to the market's exit.

P.V. stepped up onto the bar platform, and placed her well-worn, hemp farmer's market bags—packed to half the handles with winter fruits and vegetables—in one of the high and cushiony, black-leather and steel bar stools next to her. Inwardly, she felt the answer raise its hand again, eager to reveal to her where in the world she could almost immediately, with sure permission, escape to—go.

The sun was streaming in from the nearby, all-glass, street entry door, and from the bottoms of the windows lining the adjacent wall. The window-tops were shuttered with semi-sheer, pale turquoise restaurant shades, illuminated by the everywhere rays into a jeweled glow. It all made her think, yearn further back, to Miami—and in the distance, Trinidad. Either would make her mum and dad brim with unspeakable relief, joy, parental pride. She knew they would not stop talking about it in forever, tearfully mail her a plane ticket, and show up at her doorstep themselves—as they had nearly just done in the days before, putting it off temporarily only at her pleading insistence. They would be empty suitcases and flat boxes in hand, housekeeper in tow, ready to pack whatever was left of her little, downsized universe up. But, she would have to rewind herself in those old, known places—return not only to the land mass, but to being just her parent's child, and not herself. And after choosing and walking in her own worlds for so long, she decided that she liked it, and was therefore unwilling to relinquish her autonomy, even in the sure, strangling grip of agony.

Glancing anxiously down at her swollen ankles, she sighed, wishing she had with her just then one of her few, saved , luxe California possessions to catch them—a tall, red velvet hassock that actually hailed from London, that was sent to her by her Mum upon the housewarming of her and Rodney's sweet, California suburban house. Her legs were so black and blue in spots, from struggling against Rodney in the nights, and their ankles puffed to capacity from both the trickle-down of that trauma and the running about with real estate clients all day. Dangling at a bar stool, they only felt worse, pulled down hard toward the earth, inflamed, ever-ballooning big. She sighed again—the pitch quality of which was the only thing that had remained in keeping with her age. Whilst heavy, it was still the sigh of a soft-spoken—and young—woman. By contrast, she *felt* 100 years old at 22—body broken, spirit beaten and lashed down into itself, soul dimmed and ever road-weary. She picked up one of the tiny, chic, flippable bar menus, and became so lost in thought again as she—almost unseeing—perused it, that she did not hear or notice him walk behind the bar.

He had been studying her for quite a few seconds, instantly taken in by everything about her. She looked like a pretty, effortless summer day, cloaked in the first frost of winter—a sweet-faced, unmade-up beauty and uncomplicated-looking, glowing all over and pink at the nose and cheeks. She was clad neck-to-knees in a glorious red floral and ivory print coat. And she had propped her tiny feet, shod in pearly-green, ballerina flat shoes, up on the rungs of the bar stool in front of her.

"D'you like red?" he asked, extending an unopened bottle of wine, startling her up from the menu. Their eyes met at the same point together and he felt shockwaves; the hairs on the back of her neck stood on end. They both instantly, decidedly, felt that they had met each other before, and their minds began reeling through old data, pictures, names, to determine when exactly their paths had crossed—and where.

He was red-haired—of a hue reminiscent of orange zest—with cornsilk blue eyes, and a strong, square jaw. His pale skin was lightly dusted at the nose with a smattering of light brown freckles, and he was reddened in patches at his cheeks and neck. He was wearing a thick, black sweater, over an open-collared, crisp, white shirt—both rolled up together at the sleeves. And in his rugged appearance of feist, he was profoundly attractive. She nodded in answer to his question, drawn into him and the curious familiarity, barely able to breathe.

"Shiraz, *on* the *house*—just for you," he said warmly, chuckling a little as, opening the bottle with a fluid motion, he poured the silky, dry, snapping red into an almost bowl-shaped wine glass. "Might as well anyway—'s actually m'lahst day 'ere, and 's pretty much the end a shift, so…"

"Oh! Um, I didn't know—I've like, never been in here be…oh—um, where are you—where are you going?" P.V. stammered, brushing strands of hair absentmindedly from her face.

He began flushing profusely red from face to tips of ears. "*Right*," he breathed to himself. "Well…I'm leaving back for 'ome—for Ustrailya," he replied aloud, pausing to laugh at himself. "Well—I guess theht lahst paht's quite obvious, right?" They both laughed at that, exchanging nervous glances with one another.

P.V. went pink in more places about her face as well, still giggling a little as she quieted. She was profoundly intrigued, curious—and it was still nagging at her as to wheresoever in the world she had first encountered him. "Australia—cool! Yeah, *figured*! Um, what—um, what makes you want to leave Dallas?"

"*Oh*. Well, some of m'mates and I were keen to open a pub together. Not back 'ome, mind you, but you know—other places the most of us 'ave lived before. We reckoned maybe we'd pop off to London and do it there, or try our hand at running a tapas place in Spain…." he paused again, laughing dryly. "Big, fanciful ideas like that, yeah? But…" he knocked on the bar, as if snapping himself out of a dream.

"But?" P.V. queried gently, her voice a breath, heart pounding, wondering what could be weighing upon him so heavily.

"Well…I decided to have a go at…well, at *seminary*, actually. Nothing vicar—um—*priest*-like or anything, mind you. Just thought…well, thought it might do me a bit a good for awhile. Think I'd actually like to teach it one day."

"W-wow," P.V. replied, shocked. She gazed warmly, compassionately, up at him. "That's...*really* cool. And...really...heavy."

"Yeah," he replied, softly chuckling a little and blushing more intensely, looking briefly down at his hands—which were nervously wiping the bar on their own, with a soft, white cloth. They were strong, and slightly reddened, with thick, padded digits. And they looked like hands that could heal, comfort, wrap around and soothing, hold. And they were ringless.

"A course, the lads've been giving me a bit a grief over it, but it's...it's what I reckon I *must* do—for me, anyway." He looked into her, searching for a nearing-compatriot.

"Yeah—I totally hear you," P.V. said, sighing audibly, absentmindedly cupping her face in her hands. She gazed up at the starlit ceiling for a few moments, lost in all that had been before leaving Cali. That unthinking motion instantly revealed her previously well-hidden wrists—both deeply gouged all around with fresh scars drying, offset by black and blue bruises in patches above them. He scanned them quickly, carefully, shocked and slightly wide-eyed. A pang of deep compassion for her began pounding, spreading throughout his chest. He silently determined that those were un-self-inflicted, unforgivable marks—as they were occurring at both wrists and all around, as if she had been tightly, forcibly restrained. And in an angry flash, he wondered who was deciding to so profoundly, in raw layers, hurt such a lovely, sweet-spirited girl. And then he saw it—her left hand at the ring finger, at its tiny juncture. Almost tattooed there for lack of sun, was the sure mark of what had quite clearly, at least somewhat recently, resided there—a tight, thick, wedding band.

"I'm Rhys," he said gently, stretching a fleshy-palmed hand toward her. He was exploring her face more directly now, waiting to catch her eyes again, so that he might perhaps discern more.

"*Rhys?*" P.V. repeated perfectly, slipping her small hand into his, a smooth against his slightly calloused, eyebrows up in query.

"Yeah—*nice*. M'Mum's 'andiwork, actually—she's from Wales. Said she was well peeved the only useful thing she could do for me was to name me properly—given as I look completely like my Dad." He chuckled a little, and she giggled in tandem, their eyes together and away from each other at intervals. He was still holding onto her hand, and was ever-so-slightly massaging the side of it with his thumb. They fell quiet again, studying each other.

"And you are?" Rhys chuckled again as he inquired, breaking the wordless stretch.

"Oh! Um, I'm..." And then P.V. called her name out loud—the whole first name, then its full middle name attachment—and then laughing nervously, the two names together. He squeezed her hand gently as she did so, and she did not let go—she let him.

"B-*eau*tiful name...names—and a bit unusual for these pahts. Y'don't *sound* like a local—though no one does anymore, I suppose. Where y'from?"

"Um, Miami…but—oh! It's—it's my parents….they're from Trinidad."

"*Oh!* Well, *right*," Rhys said, brightening further, grinning, eyes all around her face, eyes, hair. "Explains a lot—name-wise and the like."

Just then, P.V.'s smartphone alarmed. She hastily slipped her hand away from his to first rummage through her tiny, pearl-hued leather clutch. She finally produced it from where it was tucked partially away—in a separate, inner compartment of her market bag.

"'Ave an appointment?" Rhys queried, searching for a reaction, more information, in the curves of her face—as P.V. had perked up even more at the sound of the alarm, suddenly full of a verve, an industrious energy.

"Y...um, I'm having a dinner party at my place. It's like, potluck, but I'm cooking. You—you should definitely come."

"I'd *love* to," Rhys said softly, leaning partially on a forearm, toward her on the bar, fishing out his smartphone from his back pocket with the other hand. "Whereabouts—and what time?" She told him the details, and he entered them into his phone with one hand, body still inclining toward her across the bar, head just inches from hers.

"What would y'like me to bring? I'm pretty 'andy in the kitchen y'know," he asked, smiling knowingly.

"Oh—n...don't cook anything. I just met...you know—I just want you to relax and be my guest." P.V. replied, blushing again profusely. "Um—as my Mum would say, 'just bring your appe-*tite*'." She glowed again, from the sweet skin of her face, after she lilted the imitation of her mum's accent, falling almost out of breath with the rush of Rhys so close to her. She could smell his cologne—a gently musky scent that was quietly, decidedly, beckoning to her.

Rhys chuckled again, repressing a strong desire to embrace and kiss her. "And *my* Mum would 'ave a cow if she heard I popped 'round a dinnah pahty empty-'anded," he teased.

P.V. laughed, nodding in a cultural agreement. "Well, okay. Um, bring…" And then she finally took a swig of the wine well breathing, the smoke and crisp coating her mouth with an unfamiliar perfection. Surprised, she took another sip again—this time, thoughtfully, meaningfully. Her tongue was lolling about in the lane of something real, and beautiful—and it was all very, very good. "Bring this," she breathed, glancing at him from above the glass. "Um...just bring a bottle of...*this.*"

It was already near the corridor of Noel, and they swayed into the buzzing, warmly-lit room, jam-packed with standing and sitting people laughing, chatting, and gesturing as they dined. Rodney, heady with hard alcohol and pills, was tipping intermittently, as he strode at the helm of the black motorcycle jacket-clad procession—his equally intoxicated road mates attempting at swaggers in his wake. They surveyed the scene like mission-bound gangbangers as they walked, clomping wide-legged in their work boots, elbows slightly out and hands at the ready, heads switching right to left sharply and back again.

Seemingly every area of space in the little, rented condo unit was caught up in the lively dinner party. There were people—women *and* men, he noted, with an anger flash rising—sitting on metallic silver folding chairs that he and P.V. did not own; on a set of cubed, cream-colored, stow away footstools from their landlords that they had not yet touched; and on large, jewel-hued, raw silkish pillows dangling with sparkling, iridescent beads all around their seams that, like the chairs, he had not yet met. And everywhere there were plates, tumblers, and wine glasses strung with chandelier-like, clear glass markers—all in various stages of empty. The air was permeated with the enticing, mingled smells of meat and herbs, and every so often too, a spicy, floral, musky cornucopia of the guests' intertwining perfumes and colognes. His stomach rumbled, and at once he felt oddly left out, uncool, made fun of behind himself, alone—and *had.* And all of that, it boiled him from the inside.

At first, there was no reaction to their presence. But by degrees, the diners began to take notice of the queue of eight baggy-jeaned men treading through slowly and deliberately—and a hush began to lay upon, spread, one-by-one within the energetic, shiny-faced crowd. Rodney studied the countenances of the partygoers as he neared the hall's turn, seeing in some a recognition that could have only come from viewing his and P.V.'s stilted wedding photos. Those were the photos framed in thick platinum, but tucked very nearly behind other, almost completely enveloping, international curios on the living room bookshelf. And then, as he rounded the corner, turning a steel-toed boot toward the alcove-entry kitchen, he saw them—together.

P.V. was slowly scrubbing the inside of a tiny, copper pot in the sink and laughing out loud. And a man—who was standing just inches away from her—was head turned to her and also laughing, whispering something to her whilst actively washing a deep and oversized, cast iron pan. The man was slightly taller than P.V., medium red-haired and of a slight build, but surprisingly had somewhat defined muscles peeking out from the edge of his navy blue polo shirt. P.V. playfully nudged the man with an elbow as she turned her head back to the sink. Grinning, the man turned back to the sink as well—returning her nudge gently with his upper arm, and bridging more distance to stand slightly closer to her, as he did so.

"*Waaaw*," Rodney uttered, startling them. They twisted quickly, almost in unison—towards each other first—hands still in the sink and holding pots. Then, necks craning uncomfortably further, they spotted him. Their jaws dropped open almost in tandem, four eyes alert and staring.

"I said, '*wow*'. *Hahaaa—hahaaa!* Now jus' *look* at dis shit, boys—jus' *look* at all *dis*," Rodney snarled, his voice quite patently wavering in a danger zone, emitting a sure threat underneath its steadiness. His crew was all around him—some behind, and others to the left and right of him, forming a loose gauntlet on all sides and back. "Dis some *shit* for *real*—ain't it boys? Some *shit* for *real*." He was crookedly smiling and nodding, glaring directly into P.V.'s eyes, deliberately icing out her companion at the sink.

Some within the crew of eight ringing around Rodney chirped up—eager for an impending confrontation—with supportive rounds of, 'Oh, *uh*-uh!' and, 'I don' *belie'* dis shit,' and, 'who da *fuck* is *dat*?' But one in particular—Rodney's number one man, his trustworthy—turned his head slightly toward Rodney, and stepped out from where he had originally placed himself, just behind Rodney's right side.

"Yo, *Rod*—whatchoo wanna *do*, man?" the number one man inquired. And turning to glance into first the eyes of Rhys, then P.V., he shook his head slowly at each, in exaggerated, marked disapproval. "Jus' say the word, bruh. Jus' say the *word*."

But Rodney raised his right hand to brace off his crony. "Good Evening, honey," he cooed stiltedly at P.V., enunciating perfectly. "I don't mean to *interrupt*. Um—why don't you introduce me to your *friend*? Your clearly, *very, very helpful* friend?"

P.V. flushed profusely all throughout her face, little hands letting go, inadvertently dropping the small pot clunking into the sink. Turning fully to face Rodney, she stammered, "R-Rhys, this is—this is...Rodney..."

"Her *husband*," Rodney snapping, inserted, keeping his gaze steadily fixed into P.V.'s eyes. Then, pointedly, he let his eyes shift to a spot in the middle of her forehead and back—into her eyes again. He began clenching and re-clenching his fists at his sides. His body was shaking, infused with yet another drug—its own, adrenaline—atop an all-throughout rage. But, despite his seething, Rodney deliberately kept his face soft, lips wryly lifting, teeth bared in an over-charm and faux delight.

"...my...husband...Rodney, um, this is Rhys," P.V.'s voice was toothpick thin, wavering then breaking, a string of increasingly frightened sounds barely above a whisper. By then, the epidemic hush careening throughout the unit had finally reached the diners near the kitchen and dining room, who found themselves blocked by the backs of Rodney and his crew.

"Hullo, Rodney," Rhys offered flatly. He cautiously, slowly pivoted after he did so, wiping his hands carefully in the kitchen towel that he had earlier haphazardly tucked into the belt of his jeans.

Rodney, eyebrows up in a flash of shock, jerked his head—chin first—in the direction of Rhys. He instantaneously recoiled, taking the man fully into his review as he did so. His right-hand man, however, smoothly rotated his head toward Rodney's again—one eyebrow raised in a challenging query. Rodney ignored his right-hand man, keeping his gaze on Rhys. "Hu-llo, *Rhys*," he responded mockingly. "Now, let me just *guess* where *you're* from?"

"Ustrailya," Rhys replied, eyes locked equally on Rodney's own.

"M-*hm*—Australia, huh? Uh-huh. That would've been my *guess*! *Hmph*. Uh—nice to meet you, *Rhys*." Rodney countered. He looked at P.V., eyes narrowing into hers, shaking his head. His upper lip curled up again, into a sneer. Then turning his head, he kept the corner of his eyes trained on P.V.'s, whilst sending his voice low and into the ear of his friend on the left. "Yo, *Jay*—text Baby an' tell him to stay in the muh fucking car—we been gone too long as it is, an' he gon' think somethin' wrong. He probably flyin' up the steps right now. An' don't tell him *shit* 'bout any a dis, ah-*ight?*" His friend to his left nodded and whipped out his smartphone, texting in thumbs as he strolled back through the gaping-mouthed crowd. The partygoers parted themselves like the Red Sea, gazing apprehensively at him as—head down—he clipped toward the door.

They stared at each other—Rodney and his crew at Rhys and P.V., and the two back—for what seemed an eternity, each locked into the gravity of the moment. The air was heavy and static with the potential of a much darker reality to storming, come. Rodney kept constant the intensity of his penetrating high beam through P.V., challenging her with raised eyebrows. His lips were crooked and smirking at her, taunting her. And Rhys was watching at the whole of Rodney in a wary readiness— eyes scanning across the row of Rodney's crew and back again, with the very same vigilance. Rodney's little militia of men stood the most of them arms folded and still, raining invisible darts at Rhys with their eyes. Some were shaking their heads slowly, conveying their disapproval. Everybody— including P.V.'s invitees, who had begun to whisper amongst themselves, and clinking, place down their plates, silverware, glasses—was waiting on Rodney. They were all of them in the room chests-pounding aware, that he was—or might indeed soon become—the snapping kind.

"Um," Rodney began again, saccharine-sweetly, and smiling, eyes dead and in the middle of P.V.'s own. "Honey—I'd like to have a word with you if I could?" Before she could protest, he walked forward, and sidling up to her, grabbed her forearm, and began forcefully propelling her out of the kitchen. She began to resist, but he leaned down and whispered gleefully, breath hot and dank with hard spirits in her ear: *"Girrrl—I'm a break dis lil' arm in front a all yo' party guests, unless you do exactly what I tell you. An' ya know I'll do it, too. Now start walkin'."* And, tightening his grip, and visibly setting his teeth, Rodney roughly yanked P.V.'s little upper arm forward, and resumed his breezy stride.

P.V. wished in a flash that Georgina and Juanita had been able to attend that night—or that she'd called the dinner party off entirely. Three of Gina's children—inclusive of Baby Seven—had fallen ill with high fevers, and there was a real question as to whether the rest of the brood had been affected. Her mind traveled back toward her quick cell phone call to Gina earlier that evening, assuming that her newfound friend was already hustling out the door with another of her fragrant, ribs-warming side dishes. Instead, P.V. was met with an anxious-voiced Deacon on Gina's phone, telling her of the sudden illness of Seven and the smallest of the three children. "It's gon' be alright, though," Deacon had assured her, struggling to steady his voice, emit it out as a calm. And then he called P.V. by name, and said, "Now, don't you worry 'bout it—we'll call you if anythang…we'll call you. Jus' enjoy yo' dinner party an' don't worry." But in the background, she could hear Gina, quiet and terrified, calling to him, whispering, "*Deacon, Deacon...*"

And Nita and Beau were back in Beaumont, jointly visiting their families before popping off to a Christmas holiday in New Mexico with childhood friends. P.V. had nevertheless felt their spirited, electric presences via texts and phone calls earlier in the afternoon. Despite it all, having already hosted a couple of the dinner gatherings, she had felt such a curious old-pro-ness—coupled with the warming presence of Rhys and the merry camaraderie from the even larger population of eager guests. Rhys had even arrived with two wine carriers full of bottles of shiraz from one vintner that he thoroughly enjoyed, for her guests—and a special bottle just for her, that he wanted her to try, from his absolute fave winery. So altogether, the night had felt as a comfortable cloak around her shoulders, that she could wear easily alone—until she'd twisted half-way around to shockingly, face a twitching, sneering Rodney.

Most of Rodney's crew began instinctively strolling back out into the hallway, clearing a permanent path to the door. Rhys seized the opportunity to attempt to save P.V.—sailing in Rodney's direction, hands outstretched to pull him back and away from her. But four of Rodney's detail stopped him—the right-hand man at their helm, who planted himself as if an isolated barrier almost directly in front of Rhys' face. Two of the crew held Rhys' arms, and another one pushed him back. With the three still pushing and pulling at him, the four then completely encircled him in all of their commotion, crushing him into the kitchen counter.

"Hold up, hold up, hold up, Australia—it's all *good*, it's all *good*," the right-hand man said, smiling playfully, as—taking over for the number three man, he placed his own hand on Rhys' chest—and stepped more evenly in front of him. But Rhys resisted, straining against the lock hold the two had on his arms. The right-hand man nodded his head approvingly, grinning. "Dang y'all—look at this mutha fucka here—got himself surrounded an' he *still* tryin' ta kick some ass." The crew erupted into laughter, hooting down into chuckling. The fourth, leaning deeply into Rhys' face like the right-hand man, observed him exaggeratedly from the peripheral, through a long, sideways gaze.

"He jus' like Baby," the fourth finally reported, teeth flashing.

The crew laughed again, but the number one man—still chortling— shook his head. "Naaaaw—Baby woulda kicked a dude's head straight in by now. Brutha woulda turned up missin' an' empty—unless a course, he had his *boys* dere to *break it up for him* an' keep him on the *livin'* end a thangs, an' shit. Uh—ain't that right, Pussy?" They all laughed again—except for Pussy, who looked, queasy, away—rubbing unconsciously at the thick bubble of a keloid scar on his forehead.

The number one man was grinning wider, ear-to-ear, palm still splayed and pushing firmly at Rhys' chest. "Look, dude—m'man jus' need to have a word. He ain' seen his wife in awhile, you know?" But Rhys pitched his head and torso forward, still struggling against the crew. "*Yo-yo-yo*, man—I *said* it's *all good*. *Dang*—you fightin' like a man who know too much. Whatchoo know, Australia?" The number one man went nose-to-nose with Rhys, mouth still grinning, but eyes glaring into him. Rhys bucked forward again—knocking the number one man back, straining out even through the forearms—trying to muscle out of the crew's backward-forward grasp.

"I *said*, it's *all good*," the number one man repeated, raising an eyebrow, the ever-present smirk disappearing rapidly from his face. "*Dang. Look*, yo—*relax* for a minute, dude. *Shit. Look*—one a yo' countryfolk be rollin' wit' us an' shit, so you ain't—you ain't *new*. So, jus' *relax*. 'Cause a dat shit, we prob'ly ain' 'bout to *hurt* you right now—unless you *wanna* be hurt right now. An' I mean—if you *do*, this right here's a great way to *start* that hurtin' kinda shit."

Rhys looked out past the crew, through a juncture between two of their shoulders, at the blur of partygoers. A terrorized murmur had taken foothold about the place. Some were at their cell phones, texting, calling—and others had raised their devices partially up into the semi-darkness, videotaping the events for evidence. Their communications activities were only a miniscule comfort to Rhys personally, as his own safety was of little concern to him. But, he felt somewhat relieved that somehow, because of their own vigilance, the partygoers might themselves be protected. And yet, he was not only horrified that Rodney and the other portion of his crew had spirited P.V. forcibly off into the hall, but frightened that they had likely dragged her out and away into the night—where she might never be found. That fear, unknowing—itself a bigger vise grip of potential, impending danger—kept his heart struggling madly against its cavity as if desperately desiring escape, and his entire body rigid and at the quick. He was already calculating the million places to haul off to next in the Dallas darkness, in the frantic search for P.V.

They most of them, Rodney's boys—who had filed out ahead of Rodney and P.V.— bounced down and stood on the well-traversed, concrete stairs. They were almost head-to-head like a canopy of trees and texting, checking their e-mails. They were all in a sole mindthink—an ominous, leather-clad gauntlet in black. And sides to the action, they were tacitly giving just enough space to Rodney for privacy, but yet making it clear that they were there for him—that P.V. wasn't safe without his blessing. As Rodney yanked her by the wrist to a space just outside their unit door, P.V. saw them—how they had arranged themselves on the stairs—so cool, nonchalant, and blocking. It was soul-crushing, clear to her that if they carried her off somewhere, no one inside would know in sufficient time. The middle of her chest scrambled into the pit of her neck and began banging, banging, banging there. She was, to the marrow of her bones, terrified.

Rodney maintained his clench about her wrist, and pulled her abruptly into a squeezing tight to him. His breath was booze-laden and hot on her ear and neck. "*Sooo—wha's goin' on up in dere, Wifey? Huh?*" Rodney's voice was low, just a hair above a whisper, and deadly. She could feel his fickle energy readying itself to snap, even unto the tiny, invisible pores about her neck and jaw. As if perceiving her heightened sensitivity there, Rodney kissed her neck slowly, pressing into it by degrees. And then he drew abruptly back, unsmiling—staring her down straight into the eyes.

"*Mmmm*—you smell so *good*, Ms. Thang! You *do*, Wifey, *honey*—you *do*. You *rea-lly fuck-in' do*. All *exotic* and *cinnamon* an' whatnot! *Mmmm*—it's *nice*, Wifey. It's *nice*. But now—let's be honest. You didn' wear all dat *nice spice* for *me*, now *did* you, Wifey—*huh*? Clearly, huh? You didn' even wear it for dem 300 mutha fuckin' *gums* you got up in our h...condo. You *really* wore all dat for yo' *boyfrien'* for later dat you got, huh? *Didn'* you, Wifey? Hah? *Didn'* you? Wha's his name again, Wifey—hah? 'Rhys'? Dat's his name? Dat's his name, Wifey? Hah?" P.V. flinched, turning her head well away from Rodney's, surprising herself in all of that strange, dangerous company, by nevertheless struggling, pushing with all of her mass against Rodney's chest.

Rodney kissed P.V. hard and gnashing on the mouth, and in sheer horror, she tried to recoil. He pulled suctioning deeply back away from her lips, to glare into her again. She darted her head away—and right to left and back—trying to avoid both his glower and another advance. "*Ha*. Got yo'self a lil' *boyfrien'—don't* you, Wifey? Lil' *Australian* boyfrien'—hah, Wifey? Hah? Uh-*huh*. Oh, he *want* you—I can see *dat*. An' I see you want him *too—don't* you, Wifey? *Simple, treacherous bitch—don't you, hah? Don't* you? Hah? *Hah*? *Girrrl*, I'll kick all da *daylight* out cha eyes—right here, right *now*—you bettah *say* somethin' fo' yo'self!"

P.V. felt the floor receding into itself, stretches by stretches. She was having difficulty concentrating—eyes, mind, blurring all happening. Then she realized that she was somehow hyperventilating, that she was in that stark, metallic zone of losing consciousness. Rodney saw her mouth breathing irregularly and shook her, jamming, back into the sick and dark of the present. "*I* see you, Wifey—*I* see you," he said gruffly. "You got a job an' I don't. Got yo' rich-ass mommy an' daddy an' I don't. An' dey got you playin' like you get ta make all da plans. Little Miss Thang. *I* see you. An' now I see you think you can jus' be havin' big ol' muh fuckin' dinner parties, an' whippin' up expensive things an' shit for 500 mutha fuckin' people, an' dat dats alright an' shit, 'cause it's yo' mommy an' daddy's money. Well, I'm a tell *you* somethin'—an' *I* ain't *playin'*, Wifey. What you 'bout ta do right now, is you 'bout ta clear all a dem 850 mutha fuckas— includin' yo' all-too-mutha-fuckin'-helpful-ass Australian boyfriend—*out* da crib, right-da-fuck *now*, Wifey. And dat includes talkin' to whoever official show up at dis door—since e'erybody in dere got a million muh fuckin' cell phones an' shit, an' probably even done called up da news by now—an' explainin' dat what all dat went down when me an' m'boys showed up was jus' a simple muh fuckin' misunderstandin'. *Now. You* get to *do* dat, Wifey— *you* get to do *all* dat—since *you* done planned all *dis* shit behind my back— an' *den* had da nerve ta invite yo' Australian-ass boyfrien' up into our *crib*. *Now. I'm* a be at da club wit' m' boys— but I'll be back. An' if *e'ery one a* dem *95,000 mutha fuckas* in dere ain't gone dey way *yo'* way, den dey gonna be gone *mine*. An' by den, dis here gon' be a *much bigger* incident dan it is already. An' you don' *want* dat, Wifey. You don' *even wanna know* how *simple* I can get—*trust* dat. Trust *dat*. Trust dat you don't wanna know 'bout *dat* kinda simple shit dese days, honey. So, I *suggest* you get yo' boozhe ass *busy*, an' get ta *clearin' out*—right *now. Right fuckin' now, Wifey.*"

And then Rodney let P.V. go, pushing her swift and slamming hard into the door—exerting all quick pressure at her wrist and waist and ribcage. His boys looked up at the sounds instinctively, in rounds, from their illuminated cell phone devices. And in a flash, as Rodney turned his face, ice-edge away from P.V. and pivoted, they were all of them—without query—stomping down the chipping, worn-out, rented condo unit steps with him, and gone.

P.V. heard the key in the door, and instantly wished that she had left with Rhys, or at the very least, either before him, with the frazzled, well-wishing stragglers, or just prior to that, with the main flock of her shell-shocked guests—all of whom had offered up their bedrooms and third bedrooms to her as safehouses for a night until whenever. She was hands still in the sink, scrubbing at the last of her big, copper pots, mind safely on re-curing her deep, anvil-heavy, cast iron pans.

"*Hiii, Wifeeey!*" Rodney called out brightly, stumbling into the kitchen, feet after feet bowing out occasionally at the ankles. He rotated his head in the air like a joystick. "*Dang,* girl—it still smell like you cooked every muh fucka wit' legs in here fo' yo' par-tay." P.V. said nothing in reply, only observing him cautiously from the periphery as she turned to begin to re-cure the heavy pans set near the stove. Rodney was incessantly sniffing, and wiping underneath his nose with the back of his hand, near knuckles to his wrist—despite the fact that there was nothing running from it. And his movements were slurry and jerky, a curious combination of reactions to still space and time.

"*Damn*," he breathed, chuckling, breaking the eerie blanket. "You clinical as *shit*—got dis whole place lookin' like nothin' e'er happened to it an' shit—like you didn' jus' have 15,000 boozhe mutha fuckas up in here ta-night, tippin' back drinks an' grub an' shit." P.V. still said nothing—but instinctively, she slowed her movements. She was a head turned slightly in Rodney's direction, to more carefully observe him—even with eyes downcast.

"What'sa matta, Wifey—you mad 'cause I know you got a *boyfriend?*" Rodney mocked, sneering intensely. His leaned with a hand bracing in the upper corner of the open doorway, but his head and body swayed occasionally, constantly missing at equilibrium. He reeked of alcohol as if he had bathed—full immersion—in it, and his eyes were bloodshot in deepening layers of red. "*Wifey got a boyfrien', Wifey got a boyfrien'—don't* you, Wifey?" he sing-songed, smirking. And then, in a punch of anger, he screamed, "I said, '*don't* you, Wifey'—*you simple bitch!*" P.V.'s whole body jumped, in sheer, unadulterated fright. Her neck, heart, core, began resonating with a thing rising up, that was shrieking to her about a danger near, present, real. Rodney sailed at her, shoving her from sideways, slamming her straight back into the counter lining the kitchen sink. Her breath was caught in the terror: she could not get herself to make a sound. She grappled nearby for one of her clean pots, but fell short of its reach as Rodney slapped her hand away, grabbing it and her other hand at their raw wrists.

"*Uh-uh, Wifeeey,*" he warned, still singing, but tone like hot steel, insides breathing heavily down at her. "'Cause if you hit me wit' somethin', it gon' be *news at 11* up in this mutha fucka ta-night *for re-al*, girl." P.V.

struggled in vain to break free of his grasp, her skin burning as it turned tightly in his palms.

Suddenly, in a straight line from one of Rodney's nostrils, a wide trickle of blood sprang out, and began to rapidly roll down to meet his lip. "*Damn*," he whispered roughly, inhaling hard. Without releasing her, he dropped his head and raised a shoulder, wiping his nose on his jacket. The slick of blood against smooth leather left a wet trail on the garment that shone, as if oozing, in the bright halogen cast of the kitchen.

"*Sooo*, let me get dis *straight*, *Wifey*," he said sharply, bending into her more whilst restraining her, head left to right, attempting to stare her straight in the eyes. "You decided you was gon' have a mutha fuckin' party in here ta-night. Oh, I see you now—I see you now. You been havin' dese lil' shindigs for *awhile* now, hadn't you? Uh-huh. Simple bitch. An'—let's see—lemme see dem eyes *good*, now, Wifey—so I can read yo' ass some more. 'Cause yo' face be tellin' me *e'rything*, Wifey— *e'rything*. I keep tellin' you, yo' ass'd be jus' *shit* at poker—a'least wit' me. *Shit* at it. Ok, ok—I see...*yo'* simple ass haven't fucked dat man yet—but I already know as a man he wanna be all up in you—an' a course, I already know *you* want *him* to be all up in *you*, too, so...*oh*—it's jus' a matter a time—dat right, Wifey? Huh? Dat's what you don' even know you really wishin', huh? Huh? Uh-*huh*. I told you-I told you-I told you—I *know* you, Wifey. I know how yo' lil' girlie head thinks an' shit, 'cause I'm all up *in* it. I'm all up in *here*, Wifey. I'm all up in *here*." And then he bent down rapidly and knocked his forehead—dead center—hard into hers. Her skull began to throb from everywhere on the inside, and she became aware of the not knowing what was next. The fear was pushing at her from deep within, heart banging against the walls of her chest.

Rodney turned his head to one of P.V.'s ears, speaking a low baritone into it, voice steady and threatening. "So, in *dat* case, Wifey—lemme tell

you what *you* gon' do—lemme tell you. You gon' call up yo' Aussie mutha
fuckin' frien', who I now know you *really* wanna fuck—matter a time, right?
An' you gon' tell him not to come back up in here no more. An' yo' *frien'*—
he all *well brought up* an' shit—he'll *listen* to you." And then Rodney reared
back, kissing her on the cheek, and returned his mouth back to her ear. His
breath was searing, wet, and flammable on her tiny canal's flesh.
"*Mmmmm*—you really do smell *good*, Wifey. I should fuck you right now. If
I wasn't so fucked up, I *would*, Wifey—I *would*. *Hahahahaha*—you *know* I
would. See—I gave you a *pass* on being fucked all up in dis kitchen, an' look
what you go an' do ta repay my muh fuckin' kindness. *Now*—one a dese
days soon—I'm a *have* ta fuck you *e'erywhere* up in here. All up on yo'
favorite pots an' shit, an' all up on dese counters. *Hahahahaha*. Just lift yo'
little ass up an' *fuck* you. *Hahahahaha*. *Huh*—I *told* ya." He leaned away
slightly, to gauge her reaction. Tears were tipping at her eyelashes and
falling slowly one after the other like rain, in splintered streams down her
cheeks. He inhaled and embraced her tighter, head heavy and balancing on
top of hers. "*Awww*, Wifey. Don't cry. Ain' nuthin' ta *cry* about—
jus'…words ta *live* by an' shit."

Still holding P.V.'s forearms in a vise grip, Rodney quickly swooped
in to kiss her. She moved her head in a wobble, attempting to dodge his
slobbering pucker, but he caught her. Mashing his mouth onto hers, he
began to press his teeth onto her teeth, to force her to lips, open. A flash
of anger quickened through him again, and he began to shake her violently,
screaming and trying to catch her ears. "*Now, don't fuck aroun' wit' me, you
simple bitch!* 'Cause I'm serious as a mutha fuckin' *heart* attack! *Yo*—if I find
out—if I find out his ass has been back up in here, it ain' gon' do *shit* for
international relations dat day, y'understan' dat? Y'understan' dat, Wifey? It
gon' be straight up *news at 5* up in here, y'heard? *Y'heard* dat? An' *dat* shit
would've been *yo'* choice an' shit. An' jus' in case—since you clearly such a
sneaky, *simple ass* bitch, wit' all dese mutha fuckin' state house dinner parties

you been havin' behin' my back—all while a brutha still outta work an' shit—if I find out you hangin' out wit' him *outside* dis crib, it gon' be dat news dey got ta *break away* for, straight up in the mornin' an' shit. An' in either instance, I'm a fuck y'all *both* up *real good* an' shit, y'heard? A brutha got all kinds a weapons—*trust.* An' ain't *nobody* gon' look pretty after all *dat*—not e'en *me*—'cause at dis point right here, I ain' got nuthin' ta lose, Wifey. Y'heard? Ain't got *nuthin'.*"

P.V. was sick to her stomach, energy flagging from flailing against Rodney. Still, she could utter no sound. He let her wrists go again, and grabbed her around the waist, encircling her in a bear grip. He kissed the side of her head at the temple, resting his chin on the top of her head. He began speaking at her in the air well above her, voice suddenly lowered and soft again. As he spoke, he swayed her in a rocking motion, side to elliptical side, like their unit's stacked washing machine agitation. And P.V. felt the nausea steadily rising, rising to meet the inside of her cheeks.

"*Mmmmmm*—you smell so *good*, Wifey," Rodney in repeat, breathed. "What you wash yo' hair wit'? Somethin' different for yo' boyfrien'? Huh? Smellin' like home cookin' an' good perfume, an' shit. *Mmmm. Huh.* Spendin' all our money—I mean, yo' *parents'* money—ta smell good for dat Aussie dude, huh? Dat Aussie dude who wanna fuck you, huh? Dat Aussie dude who I *know* yo' lil' ass wanna *fuck. Huh.* You really think I'm a let y'all do all dat? *Hah?* Mm-*mm*, Wifey! Mm-*mm*! Now—you was a virgin when I met you, an' I was yo' first an' only—so, we *been* through all *dat*, right? So now, *why* den, am I gon' give up my *princess*, my lil' Trinidaddy *virgin* an' shit—who I had ta *break in*—up ta some random, foreign-ass mutha fucka cleanin' pots all up in my crib, *huh?* I mean, I been *trainin'* you, *teachin'* yo' ass things. Teachin' you how ta please a man in *bed*—how ta please *me*, an' shit. You should be *grateful* ta me for all dat shit, an' you should learn ta *like* dat shit. I mean, *shit*—huh? You take thangs *way too personal*. Fragile as a mutha fuckin' *doll* an' shit—Wifey, you act like a mutha fuckin' *doll*."

Rodney kissed the top of P.V.'s head again, and rearing back, stared fixedly into her eyes. "I mean—but do I *hit* you?" he suddenly asked, from nowhere. "Do I *hit* you an' shit? I 'on't *hit* you. I 'ont' *hit* you, Wifey—do I *hit* you? *No*. It's jus' *sex*—it's jus' *sex* an' *buck freaky, fun* shit. *Hmph.* You so little! All up in yo' head—you so *little*! Don't you know dat? It's jus' *sex*. You ain' no woman—no *grown ass* woman, anyway. You a—you some kinda *girl*, Wifey. Some kinda...I 'on't even *know*. You got ta learn ta *enjoy* all dat shit we be doin'. You got ta learn ta *handle* dat shit. An' if you cain't, I 'on't know—but I ain't divorcin' you. An' I sho as hell ain't gon' leave you alone. I mean, basically, you jus' *fucked* if you cain't handle dat shit. *Shit*—I 'on't even know all what I'm sayin' right now, Wifey—but I know I mean e'ery las' word, so don't get it twisted. Don' fuck aroun' an' git yo'self hurt later, either. 'Cause I *will* hurt you, Wifey. I *will* hurt you. I *will do* dat shit. If you think I hurt you before, *huh*—jus' *try* my ass. *Huh.*"

Rodney shook P.V. roughly, once, sealing the threat into her with a glassy, darkened gaze. She was limp in his hold, hardly breathing and tear-streaked. He smiled, body softening. "Oh, *Wifey*! A brutha high *for real*, right now—*hahahahaha*. You know dat, right? You know a brutha high right now, right? I be eatin' pills an' shit for breakfast like, e'eryday, *all* day. *Hahahahahaha.* I'm like a five-year-ol' wit' a stash a muh fuckin' Easter candy, an' shit. *Hahahahahaha.* Though—dat's not what's fuckin' me up good right *now*, Wifey. *Hahahahahaha.* Dat's not it, Wifey. *Ahhh. Huh.* Lemme tell you somethings, Wifey. Lemme tell you somethings while we still got time. Wifey—my *Wifeeey.*" Rodney tightened his arms, and then let go his grasp. He placed a long, stretching hand on either side of P.V. on the counter, bending down again to look at her face, boxing her in with his towering torso.

"See, now, Wifey—you made life extremely difficult tonight, wit' yo' simple ass, wit'out e'en knowin' about it. 'Cause, see—dey's somethin' you *'on't* know. We got a Aussie dude dat hang out wit' us, too. *Yeah*—we actually *do*! All up in Dallas, of all muh fuckin' places in da worl' an' shit—I *know*! Now, let me tell you how I met dis muh fucka—an' he a stand-up guy, he really is. I like him an' shit—he crazy as hell—but I like him. Matta fact—I like him *'cause* he crazy as hell. *Hahahahaha.* Dat's jus' how I been feelin' dese days, Wifey—ya know? Okay, okay—lemme see…see, me an' da boys was out doin' shit y'on't need ta know about…but let's jus' say dis, let's jus' say dis—we had taken in a little gentlemen's entertainment dat evenin', dat still was goin' on after hours an' shit. By da way, dat's why I be wearin' da condoms wit' you an' doublin' dem up an' shit, an' want you ta be doin' dat diaphragm an' shit—*dat's* why. Y'feel me? I mean, *huh*—my middle name is 'no catch, no carry' an' shit. Y'heard? *Huh.*" P.V. shuddered against the counter, blocked in by the solid and heat of Rodney's trunk, in a pocket without air. She felt the sudden urge to vomit at him.

"*A-nyway*," Rodney continued, oblivious to the change of shades in P.V.'s face. "All of a sudden, some shit broke out—shit jus' be breakin' out at dese places sometimes, Wifey, especially da ones I gotta go to now, since I ain' got no job an' shit. It be rough. *Hahahahahahaha.* Anyway, anyway—so, when da shit broke out, dey kicked all our asses out into da street, right? *Now*—e'erybody had had a lot a e'erything by dat point, see. So mutha fuckas was just swingin' an' fightin' for no reason, an' shit. *Now*—turns out, *some* a dem mutha fuckas was, in fact, Australians an' shit. *Now*—I wish I had a *known* dat. Otherwise, I might a been da muh fuckin' recipient a world-ass peace dat night, 'cause I wouldn'a let my boys let things git so outta hand wit' dem—on account a none a us was in good enough condition to be *fightin'* like dat—y'feel me? 'Cause I had heard way back in da day—an' I mean, *waaay* back—dat you gotta watch it when you be fightin' wit' 'em. 'Cause dey asses don't wanna stay down—if it's on, it's *on*—an' you best be *ready*. So, anyway, anyway—I clocked dis one big-ass Australian mutha fucka straight up in his mouth, *pow*—mutha fucka was bigger an' taller dan *me* an' shit. I 'on't e'en know what a brutha was thinkin', but I was high—'an I was tryin' to help m'boys out an' shit. Anyway, he *did* clock a brutha back, an' let's jus' say a brutha cain't remember now some a da shit dat went on directly *after* dat—partly on account a da fact dat a brutha found himself on the asphalt temporarily, hopin' dat big white baller hadn' knocked out my beautiful-ass white *grill* an' shit. I mean, it's all about da teeth, Wifey. Y'*know* I takes care a m'*teeth*. So, y'know *I* couldn' be havin' *none* a dat mess!"

Rodney tipped his head to one side, eyes away and up, lost in reliving the night. "Now, now, anyway—when I *fin'lly* come to, I'm seein' dat like, three a m'boys had held dat Aussie dude off an' shit, an' had dragged me nicely ta da side, so a brutha could, y'know, *rest* a while, *hahaha*. But den, one a dem, who looked like a mutha fuckin' infant in da face—no fuck— like a twelve-year-ol', like a baby-faced assassin an' shit...*dat* one starts wailin' on one a *our* little runts, like *bambambambambambambam*! An' dat shit was sooo...I mean, *spectacular* an' shit, Wifey! I mean, *frightenin'* right— 'cause he coulda *kilt* his little ass an' shit, so a course we couldn' let him jus' go on *indefinitely* wit' all dat shit, all up our boy...but I was like, 'hol' up, hol' up—*I* wanna learn to fight like dat an' shit, though!' I mean, *bambambambambam*, Wifey—all while sittin' all up on a brutha *stomach* an' shit! *Dat* was like some kinda *Greco-Roman*-ass shit! It was muh fuckin' beau...I mean, *I* for *one* was a enraptured muh fucka. Couldn' stop starin' an' shit. It looked like a muh fuckin' *cartoon*..." Rodney paused, shaking his head slowly in a revisited disbelief. The sensation of nausea had transformed, heightened to a desire to allow all things to go black, and P.V. was therefore certain that a crashing unconsciousness would soon topple and slump her over one of Rodney's endless, blocking arms.

Rodney all of a sudden hugged P.V., squeezing her body hard into his, smashing her head against his chest. "...An' den—an' den Wifey, I was like...I was like...'oh snap, though—we gotta help our *boy*, yo.' I mean *damn*. Muh fuckin' *entertainin'*, regardless. An' we was all standin' aroun' thinkin' da same thing. Seriously. We all...we all jus' stopped fightin' wit' each other, it was like, all in slow mo' an' shit...fists jus' on pause in mid-air an' shit—an' we was all jus' starin' an' laughin' at all dat. His boys, our boys. I mean, *dat* baby-faced mutha fucka was on his *knees*, an' *our* boy was on da *groun'* an' *he* was jus' a straddlin' our boy an' jus' a beatin' his head into a little *pulp* an' shit. I mean, frightenin', *for real*—but dat shit was sooo *entertainin'*, dat we mutha fuckin' made up wit' all dem Australians, an' e'en adopted dey little sociopathic twelve-year-old. He really like, *25* an' shit, I think. So we roll wit' dem sometimes, an' he basically always be rollin' wit' us. We call him 'Baby', an' now we call our boy he almost done kilt, 'Pussy', *hahaha*. An' now I cain't e'en *look* at *our* lil' fuck in da face an' shit—'cause he *is* such a *pussy*. He's such a *pussy*, Wifey. Such a muh fuckin' *pussy*. *Now*. Dat Baby mutha fucka truly *is* crazy—like I said dat's why I like da dude—an' so, when you had his countryman all up in here tonight wit' yo' fuckin' boozhe-ass party, we had ta try ta keep *Baby's* crazy ass in da car. I mean, y'feel me? I 'on't know *what* woulda happen between *dem* two ta-night, 'cause Baby crazy. Baby mighta jus' decided ta kill all a us an' den roll on home, an' shit—*hahahahaha*. Dat's a joke. Dat's a *joke*, Wifey. Well—*kinda*. Seriously. But I mean, seriously—it's jus' no tellin' how complicated dat mess coulda gotten. An' I mean—all behind *yo'* simple ass."

And then Rodney suddenly unhinged from P.V., stepping backwards with a force, letting her go. She at once doubled over, wheezing uncontrollably—one hand grasping at her back, which was throbbing in excruciating pain. "Anyway, anyway—I gotta be out. I 'on't got *time* ta be...jus' remember—news at 5, Wifey. Mutha fuckin' *news at 5*. Ahh-*iiight?*" Smiling eerily, Rodney almost lost his balance as he pivoted away, trudging out of the kitchen. He began sing-songing again as he departed, chuckling as he staggered against gravity. "Tell yo' Au-ssie frien' bye-bye—*bye-bye*, Wifey-*Wifeeey*! As *soon* as mu-tha fu-ckin' *pooo-ssiii-bllle*! O' I'm-a have ta *deeeal* wit' his *aaass*—an' den, I'm-a have ta *deal* wit' *youuu*! No pret-ty for no-body, *biiitch*! It's yo' *choice*, 'cause I'm-a bru-tha a-bout *choi-ces*! Re-mem-ber daaaat! Re-mem-ber dat shit, *Wifeeey*! *Huh. Hahahahahaha!* Ha-*ha*! See-ya when-I see-*yaaa*, Wifeeey!" And, still chuckling, he stumbled around the corner, towards the little rented condo unit door. He pulled it hard closed, a sudden gust of wind helping to shut it firmly behind him, without looking at it as he did so—and without looking back.

The doorbell rang, but it startled no one. Through the blinds, the sky was cadet blue, deepening in the distance to a murky grey, and listless. P.V. was on her hands and knees, stretching her little body across the kitchen tile, retrieving the assortment of vegetables that Rodney had just unceremoniously dumped out from one of her organic farmer's market bags. It was Saturday, and he had just returned late that morning from what looked like everywhere dark and dubious, having left since Wednesday. He was bedraggled, hungover, and seemingly more, and exhausted to a look of hollowness. Rodney's gait, too, was groggy and teetering, as if navigating the deck of an intermittently tilting ship. He had stood there watching P.V., who transitioned into nervously unpacking her fresh dinner party finds from her large, hemp farmer's market bags. And then, in a nanosecond, he snapped—knocking empty pots, lids, and cooking spoons to the floor in a clearing motion, from the stove and nearby countertops. He breathed in a heavy, wheezing, asthmatic fashion as he created the calamity, saying nothing. When P.V. grabbed up one of her market bags, clutching it to her chest, Rodney lunged—still unspeaking—tearing it from her hands and upturning it near her face, high above the floor. She backed away as far as she could, into the 'v' of a counter juncture, clasping her buttoned-up cardigan further closed with one hand, clamping the other hand around her own tiny bicep, to block her chest. But Rodney surprisingly pivoted wildly and stumbled out into the passageway. Wheezing louder still—and on each uptake—he waded into the dining room and grabbed one of the contemporary, cream-upholstered dining room chairs. He was dragging it back to the passageway just outside the kitchen—onto the portion of floor that led to the bedroom, that ran past the living and the dining rooms. And the only sounds then were those of his pulling breathing, and the screeching of the faux mahogany chair legs across the faux dark wood floor. He sat down on the chair spread-eagled, long back to its high one.

Rev. walked with purpose into the little rented condo unit behind P.V., black fedora hat in chubby hands—which he had immediately taken off before entering, in a gesture of Southern respect. The strained look on P.V.'s face at the threshold had driven a shock of constricting alarm into his intestines and skyward up, into his chest. As he treaded the hallway, he could at first hear only the hard mark of his own dress heels, followed by the fullness of the rest of his heavy footsteps hitting the faux floorboards. P.V.'s sounds commenced just after—tread like slippers, a tissue-quiet rustling behind him and across the room.

Rodney was still sitting on the dining room chair that he had placed squarely in the middle of the kitchen-to-bedroom passageway. He was back to the living room space, legs outstretched and akimbo, in the motorcycle stance he used to sport back in L.A. as he zipped—seemingly free in spirit—through lanes. Rev. took a long, slow look down at him from behind. Rodney was black woolly hair slightly curling, but clumped unevenly about his head and dull—clearly having neither been washed recently, nor cut, piked, or greased. His green polo shirt was profoundly wrinkled and blood-stained at the back right shoulder, and its collar was crumpled and dog-eared, unconvincingly, up. He was clad in light khaki pants that were blood-splattered and streaked with glitter and oil stains. And upon closer look, they were crusted in places with what looked like the remnants of spilled take-out—flakes of dried, yellow mustard; tiny, bright pieces of red pepper; and the like. A scan to Rodney's feet revealed that they were ashen, unbathed-looking, and half-slid into worn, brown leather flip-flops. And he was hands in pockets slouched in the seat, head tipped to one side and staring at nothing. All about him reeked of cheap cigars, deep fat fry, and some sort of heavy, head-splitting, drugstore women's perfume or body splash. The funky smells melted jarringly together to form a thick, but invisible, molecular halo around him—which knocked away at the nose of anyone near, but not of, them.

"*Rod, Rod, Rod,*" Rev. said low and raspy, placing a hand on Rodney's right shoulder, just above one of the groupings of dried blood stains. "Where you *at*, my brutha? Where you *at*?" Rodney lifted his neck with a laboring effort. Wincing, he looked up at Rev. peripherally, eyebrows raised in query. "In here," Rev. clarified, tapping the side of his own temple. "Where you *at* in *here*?"

"Who…awww, *maaan*! You dat…ain't you dat-dat *street* pastor? 'Rev.'? Awww…*huh. Maaan*! I cain't *belie'* dis *sh*—how *you* get up in here, *man? Awww...*" Then Rodney dropped his head and shaking it, sighed, a weighted exhale pushing out all protest from him. And without further prompting, he answered Rev.'s question. "I 'on't *know*, man. I on't *know*." His voice, rustling from all the wildness of the nights out, broke into quivering, simmering with the beginning of true tears. He pulled his hands abruptly out of his pockets, slapping them to his face to hide the falling water. As he did so, two unused, attached condom packets fell out of his right hip pocket and onto the floor. He seemed oblivious to them, but immediately upon seeing them, P.V.—who had planted herself several paces away, but in view of him—stepped abruptly backwards, hands grasping at the air for support behind her. Rev. too, leaned backward and away, but circled around to be more fully at Rodney's right side. His smooth, dark hand still rested squarely on Rodney's shoulder.

"My brutha," Rev. spoke into a sigh, straightening his arm and firmly squeezing Rodney's shoulder, pinching skin to bone. "*You* gon' have to come wit' me tomorr'. 7:30 a.m.—so we can beat the gridlock—in time for 9:00 a.m. services. *Church*, my bru-tha—*church*. No 'no's', no 'I 'on't knows', no 'maybes'—y'hear me now? I'm straight up takin' you to *The House* for the *Word* tomorr'—period, *full stop*. I *would* take you to *my* church, but I already planned to have a guest preacher hold it down there for me an' *Vernetta* tomorr', 'cause Pastor J. *himself* gon' be at The House, back from tour, layin' down the Testimony an' usherin' in The Spirit—and you *know* that's *exactly* what all you *need*, my *brutha*."

"*Aagh*," Rodney responded softly, like a child half-heartedly expressing its disgust. Flinching, he swiftly turned his head away. But his eyes rested their glance on the kitchen floor. One of P.V.'s organic farmer's market bags was upturned and flop-handled on the faux travertine tile. Heads of cabbage, tomatoes, and other rotund produce were frozen after momentum like billiard balls—separately and in pairs—at the cessation of their rolling journey, the smaller ones wedged partially under cabinets. Eyes still down, Rodney rotated his head, following the gleaming, wood laminate planks of the passageway floor, to the area just in front of P.V. His eyes took in her petite, tan feet. They were slightly swollen at their tops from the earlier of the day spent clipping stall to stall at the farmer's market. And they were clad in shiny, grey, pearlescent ballet flats—that he recognized from back in California. He kept his gaze on them for a moment, recording how all was so whistling clean, shiny—the faux kitchen floor, the faux passageway floor, and P.V.'s years-old, itty-bitty bow-tipped shoes. He inhaled as much air as he could and sighed again, almost noiselessly and deliberate—slowly, letting out the whole world. Silent, he looked away again. And with all of that, Rev. knew he had him.

"Mm-*hm*. My brutha, I'm 'on tell you ag'in—7:30 a.m. tomorr'," Rev. repeated, clapping Rodney's shoulder. "An' you *best* be ready. 'Cause you got an appointment wit' *Jesus* tomorr', Rod—an' you can run from e'erythang an' e'eryone else in yo' life, but you cain't run from *The Lawd*, an' that's a *fact*, my brutha—that's a hun'red percent *fact*. *Hmph*. An' lemme tell you somethin' *else* I know, Rod. I know The Spirit gon' *work* you tomorr', my brutha—that's what I *know*. Y'heard that? *Hmph*. An' you might a heard that I ain' never late, so I *suggest* you git yo'self togetha nice an' *early* tomorr', my brutha—nice an' *early*, y'heard? 'Cause—man to man? You fixin' to git *worked* by dat Spirit tomorr', brutha—*worked*. An' then, all this..." he swept at the air in a 360 all around Rodney with his other hand, just inches from Rodney's face. "...All this *madness* gon' *quit*, y'un'erstand that? It gon' *quit*, my brutha—'cause you gon' *quit* it, Rod. In the Name a The Lawd, my brutha, you gon' lay all this madness *down*."

This time, the words fell onto Rodney and were received, first by an ever-so-slight nod forward—that eventually came back again, into a consistent, slow bob. "Ahh-ight...ahh-ight...*dang*," he said pensively. He dropped his head a little, clasping his long fingers together in his lap like a school child. And in that circle, he half-laughed—a dry, hollow sound—skull rocketing up with its joyless motion, then shaking side to side. "*Ha.* You a persistent grey-eyed muh fu...*bruh*—know dat, Rev.? *Y'know?*"

"Mm-*hm*. Well, like the Good Book says, my 'testimonies are sure'—and I know The Spirit Led me to be invited to have this *visit* wit' you today, my brutha. Now I'm fixin' to run along—I got *thangs* to do now—but I'm 'on be back here tomorr'. 7:30, my brutha—remember that. Don't be late." He reassuringly—but firmly—squeezed his fingers deeply into Rodney's shoulder, and then his hand left it completely. "P.V.," he added, nodding his respects at her before replacing his hat, "don't you worr' about a thang now, y'hear? I'm 'on take care a thangs. I'm 'on take care a all a it. I'll let myself out." And with that, he pivoted, clipping across the laminate firmly—more confidently than when he came—and closed the door with an unintended half-slam behind him.

But after Rev. left, Rodney was deeply ashamed to his belly in the sight of P.V., and both a strange amusement and an equal anger began welling up in the middle of his chest, into the back of his throat, radiating its white-hot energy out across his face and ears. But for the first time, he didn't know immediately what to say. And P.V. was afraid to move, dumbfounded at all that she had witnessed. She remained rooted, with her little ballerina flats in ballet second position, hands quiet—one hand clasped on a wrist behind her. She watched at Rodney like a school girl on a museum field trip, viewing a curious exhibit, staring wild-eyed—but fixedly—at his bowed head, lowered temple.

All was silent for the longest of times, sounds creeping into the blanket around them from the outside—car horns, traffic, people loudly yelling and laughing in the parking lot below. And then, Rodney's head jerked up.

"Why you open da door to dat *giant ass*, muh fuckin' negro?" he queried half-jokingly, suddenly regaining himself, looking straight up and over at P.V., and trying to rise from the chair. "*Shiiit*. Lookin' like a big muh fuckin' grey-eyed country bear an' shit, all up in mah damn house. *Now*, I gotta go ta *church* wit' his big ol', giant country *ass*—an' listen ta all dat carryin' on I heard dey be doin' o'er dere an' shit." He began laughing at and to himself, the partial anger having been temporarily switched out for a full-on amusement. But at the tail end of his mirth, his aggression resurfaced—as stealthily and swiftly as it had bubbled up.

"*Bitch*," he snarled at P.V. "*Hmph*. You shoulda known dat I wouldn' be all dat *wild* about dat giant owl flyin' all up into my house. *Hmph*. Wit' his muh fuckin' x-ray-grey eyes an' shit. Ya *know* a brutha hates two things—number one, strangers all up in my crib, *right, Wifey?* An' number two—an' you should already know dis—*church. Shiiit*." And flashing a mischievous grin, he stood up on what looked like foreign feet, swaying

140

unsteadily. "*Huh.* I'd rather be chillin' up in here tomorr', fuckin' you *real good* instead, Wifey. *Real* good. *Huh.* Wit' yo' *fine* little ass—come 'ere, Wifey."

P.V. instinctively darted sideways. She was hoping to—in Rodney's clearly weakened state—dash past him, beyond the kitchen and around the corner, to unscathed, out of the little, rented condo unit door. But, in a half-shaky lunge and stride, he was already directly in front of her—and, still strong in his muscle-driven hands, grabbing at her palms-out-and-protesting arms. And then he began pushing—grinning down, eyes squint and flashing. He was pushing and pushing and pushing her rigid, resisting little body back, down the faux-floored passageway, into the doorway of their—his—ever too-nearby bedroom.

He was Cali Rodney gone and a desperate thing in his place and raging, all drowned in a multichemical new birth. His eyes were wide, wild, and darting—whites shot up with blood, pupils taking in too much of the all and everywhere. He was an almost visibly steaming head propped on top of a jerking, lurching body, each aspect of his physical mechanisms operating as if rough-wired separately. The mouth was sputtering, going on and on and on to itself into ramble, laughing occasionally at something unseen, a brittle cough and razor-like wheezing rounding out its utterances. And his now scrawny, endless arms spanned out to tap each at a wall every few seconds for balance, in attempts to steady the whole unsteady thing down—and through the hallway.

He saw P.V. sitting there on the dark wood laminate, living room floor—a little dressed-up baby doll to him. Her legs were straight out, tiny tan toes unpainted, and she was all flounced in a pretty, a-line, magenta-on-navy floral dress. A new pair of coordinating, navy-colored high-heels stood respectably and erect, like a mommy's once-a-month Sunday shoes, at her side. Upon seeing her, taking her in, Rodney exclaimed, "*Hah!*" It was all that he could utter for a moment, amidst the madness and mad talkings whirling within and without his tremor-ridden head.

P.V.'s pamphlets from the ob/gyn were unfolded in various stages, a pointing, pastel-and-print all around her. She was at reading about rape, reading about domestic violence, numb and numbing and steadily reading. At the sight of him she took to shaking, fear programmed—set everywhere—in her bones. And she scrambled, tried to crab-crawl urgently away from the approaching monster and onto her feet. But the glasses of Rhys' shiraz that she had poured herself for anesthesia, instead of the Sunday-typical breakfast tea, made it more difficult to do so. Finally able to brace without sliding on the contemporary, cream settee, she brought herself—shuddering up—to her feet. She clipped her half-full goblet with a frantic hand as she rose, and it jostled, but did not fall. The liquid within it started Time, as it began to shift, sway in the glass. Rodney saw the wine catching the glorious, sun rays of Sunday streaming in from the window. The liquid was lit golden and in halves, tipping, swirling—left and back, around to the right. And for a moment, he was mesmerized by it.

Then suddenly, Rodney was forward and P.V. was backward, the breath sucked from her and all air. She jerked her body to twist away—a quick, swinging pivot—feet still in full step backward, away. Her eyes were panoramic, capturing his own, then snapshotting his everything, unflinching. His hair was unruly again, and dotted with winking bits of stripper glitter and patches of beige body makeup. And the fumes coming up from his head, jacket, skin within were made of stale cigarettes in layers and repeating—it was nauseating, churning, burning to the eyes, and it made hers water, tear, run. But he was gleeful, playful, a big kid dizzy, unable to be halted.

"A *baby—f-f-f...*have a *b...aby*," he said, word stuck but mouth still grinning loopily, his whole body lunging for her.

"*Bab...*? We—we can't afford that!" P.V. terrified, grasping at any straw, strenuously pleaded. She reflexively dodged his grasp, leaning a lightning quick away from him and hurtling herself backward, petite form all of a sudden illuminated by the bright white rays of the new day.

Rodney looked at her, startled a bit—even through his fog—by the speed at which she had avoided him. "N—a *baby*." he stressed, a confusion washing over his face.

And then came an exclamation from his throat, face brightening in tandem, as he remembered something. "Oh!" He was searching, pinching through his pockets, but his hands were shaking too much to hold, produce, anything from them. P.V.'s face was wild with anxiety, she was breathing shallowly, body rigid and waiting for him to lurch again. She looked at him queryingly. "X," he explained, words slurring. "Have X— Ec..stasy. Ec-stasy for *you, you, you*. Ecstasy for *you*—an', *me*! *Hahahahaha*! Oh..."

P.V. recoiled, fear and nausea hurling up into, blazing, her esophagus. She backed away gingerly, foot by careful foot, with the intent of retreading toward—and out of—the unit door. Rodney tried to follow in a stride, reaching again into a jacket pocket as he did so. But in his fumbling haste, he pulled out the entire contents of the pocket, including the lining of itself. Uh-oh!" he exclaimed like a child, as a colorful sprinkling of pills of various shapes and sizes fell down from his dangling, white pocket patch, and into air. He watched the pills free fall, hit ground, roll the some of them across the dark, faux wood floor. He was so plainly enraptured, entranced by them—their shape, size, motion. "Oh," he breathed. "That's so...ohhh...I see...I see."

Suddenly, he snapped his neck up, staring at P.V. wide-eyed. "Are you a elephant? Are you a elephant, Wifey?" he cried. "You look jus' like dat man inside dat elephant!" P.V., frightened to the hairs on the back of her neck, shook her head slowly, warily continuing to pace backward by placing an unsteady foot slowly—one by one—behind her.

"Oh," Rodney said, in a voice soft and crestfallen, looking down. He muttered something to himself, and gazed up at her again. "So high—so high—can't *see* you, so high! So tiny, Wifey—*dis* tiny! You sooo *tiny*!" Then he lunged for P.V. once more, and this time—she screamed. She was hearing her own voice for the first time profoundly, and at its echo wondered frantically if anyone in the units nearby would hear her, too.

"Oh!" he shouted, and dipping into the other pants pocket, shakily pulled out a pinch of something, and slapped it into his mouth— swallowing it visibly painfully, with great difficulty. And then—it happened. Eyes wide, wide, wide, his face began twitching, contorting—and a hand to his neck, straining against something, he motioned to her—begging for something. He seemed as if he were trying to form that name—the one that he had slathered her with, that thing, that 'Wifey', as his lips kept coming together constantly in a blowing motion, seemingly laboring at mouthing a wordless 'W'.

"*Pallavi*," P.V. heard someone say loudly, firmly. "Pallavi *Victoria*." Goose-bumps prickled both arms, and she gasped, audibly. Hands clamping themselves on her own mouth, she realized that it was *she* who had just spoken.

Eyes widening to a circumference larger still, Rodney's countenance appeared stunned, then in a flash, it intensified, to the look of a child's deep hurt—by something he was seeing behind her. Then, his face softening to a melancholy, he fell backwards—down, down, down, into thud. His long, scrawny body knocked over the nearby faux wood occasional tables and their contents as he fell. And he stared up, up at P.V. blankly, from his newly-created living room floor debris—body splayed across the matter—a trickle of foam oozing from one crusty, desiccated corner of his half-open mouth.

P.V. was rooted. She was rooted there from her ankles pulling down, not feeling her feet, body in a stance. A shiver was beginning from her neck and traveling to her shoulders, then it reversed its egress to all about her head. She was eyes to the fixed eyes of Rodney, gasping for her own breath but not realizing it, a statue frozen at shuddering attention.

After a moment grounded there, she instantly felt, but did not see, something whirling cyclonic in front of her. It was a beingness, a presence—a somethingness anxiously exerting, pressing into her mind and the middle of her chest, seven times a thought: *sorry sorry sorry sorry sorry sorry sorry.* Her own spirit perceived it to be Rodney, his soul as if still packaged in its recently fallen form—tall—and craning down in front of her. And he was not alone.

There was another presence with him, by his side, she discerned. It was equally invisible—and observing her, but somehow, already knowing her. The second beingness was a thick, powerful, force-filled thing, wide and towering well above Rodney. And it seemed as if it were expectantly waiting—for something.

And then in an instant, the presence and Rodney's presence parted each almost to one side of P.V., yet still in front of her—and suddenly, the living room window lit up, almost blindingly. The window was all rays within and emanating from its panes—fat, full, and streaming with solar energy. A highway of visible light, embedded with a twinkling stardust, stretched out toward P.V. from it. Reaching her, it rocketed up and became conical rings—warm, seeking, and intense. The rings began at her head, opening down to hoop her entire body, pulsing a soothing healing from mind to soul to flesh. And offshoots of energy within the progressively widening, cycling spheres laid loving and reparative upon her wrists and all bruised places—sealing them down from within, solidifying their cellular foundations.

And she felt, kept perceiving, the presence and Rodney's, the presence and Rodney's—their all invisible, yet spiritually tangible, navigating and knowing entities. And then the presence telescoped up, up, up—as if beyond the ceiling—and still unseen, simultaneously waved out into tiers, pushing at the air near her in all directions, as it did so. It continued spontaneously unfurling—accompanied by an audible, loud crackling and rustling as if the sound of leaves or pine needles forming and stretching out in large quantities—as it grew. And then the presence, it revealed itself: it was in the form of the ghostly outline of a massive, towering pine tree—its endless rows of transparent, white branches and thick, almost fluorescent trunk occupying the entire half of the little, rented condo living room space. Rodney's presence, by contrast, manifested as if the flickering apparition of a child in grey scale, standing and staring—enraptured—up, up, up, at the very top of the tree. And his presence, it kept dwindling rapidly and regressing in chronological form, suddenly dwarfed and toddling well beneath the gaseous, lower branches of the pine. Ultimately shrunken in stature to the appearance of a baby, his presence suddenly wobbled slightly back and flopped down to sitting. Then, his spirit, it giggled brightly, tiny ghosted hands eagerly reaching out to hug at the base of the tree. It was as if he were once again nearing infancy, in demeanor and dimension—and Time. And then in the wisp of a nanosecond, without more, they were both—the tree presence and Rodney's presence—up, to the ceiling up, and skyward, through the beaming window, and gone.

It was 7:17 a.m., and Rev. was outside in his well-ridden but gleaming, white U.S.-make pickup truck. He was top-to-toe clad in crisp

black-and-white pinstripe—thick fedora hatband and three-point pocket
square coordinating—black wingtips and gold watch glinting in the
everywhere sun. A heavy man breathing heavily, he waddled across the
blacktop. His eyes were ever-alight and purposeful, chin out in a grace-
filled jut—he looked like Sunday morning.

But, as he neared the building, with its open stairwell—crossing over
from blacktop to concrete—he was knocked, head to knees, with a sharp
and searing abdominal pain. It took his breath from deep and exhaled it,
returning it back shuddering and shallow. And a nausea up, up, up sprang
from his belly to his throat too quickly, as he struggled to toddle over to
the stair railing to brace himself. He cradled the weathered, metal railing
like a winded child, grateful for its comforting cool against his cheek and
grounding smell of iron. Sweat began to pour from underneath his hat and
heavily, sopping every hair. And through the breaks of dimmed light
coming through at the 'v' of an elbow, he realized that he was also having
difficulty seeing. His mind reeled temporarily in a wondering, as to why he
was so quickly, profoundly ill. But, he was determined because of
Rodney—driven by his promise to church him to save him. So he pressed
on upward, foot after foot, hand over hand to the condo mountain
reaching. He was heaving hard and wheezing, each cement landing a
turning blur. And he could feel gravity dragging down on his intestines,
trying to suck them slow and steadily into below and below and below the
earth.

Several streets away, Rhys picked up his cell phone, mind deeply on
P.V. In the maelstrom of the dinner party events, and the aftermath of
comforting her and helping her clear the unit of the wild-eyed diners and
kitchen-full of soiled wares—whilst begging to stay, to not leave her to the
return of an amped-up Rodney—he had forgotten his jacket. He pressed
her contact field, and the ring continued three times, before—voice

wavering—she answered. And then she told him what had happened that day, and Told him too, of all the terrors of the days and nights beforehand.

When Rev. finally reached just near the top landing, he stopped, feet still on opposite stairs, lungs straining to grab at pieces of air from his shallow, in-out-in-out mouth open wide. His belly and all insides were burning. He rested on his hands, cheek sliding, wet skin on wet skin, the dank smell of sweat salt and cologne mingling. A long, cooling breeze hit him from the right.

And, a beat later, he heard in his head—round and round encircling—*spiritual sickness sickness spiritual sickness sickness spiritual sickness.* Something then whispered within to him, telling him to look up. Panting, he raised his head, and saw Rodney and P.V.'s condo unit door—half-open, the white light of the sun's rays bouncing off the smooth of the visible patch of floor inside. And he saw the blurred shadow of someone moving across its faux wood, and heard the attendant *clomp, trip, clomp, clomp* of what sounded like shaky pacing in high heels. The person's words were muffled to his inwardly pounding ears, but he could hear her voice talking to someone, anguished and bleating, rising and falling at intervals. He sighed and straightened up his body, mind intent on coaching his matter up the one last stair.

But just then, a large, black dog appeared in front of the door unit perpendicular to P.V. and Rodney's. Rev. had not heard it initially approach, and the skin on his arms prickled immediately at the sight of it. It seemed to have literally come from the thin, because the door behind it was not open, neither had anyone rounded the stairwell corner beyond that door—in form or voice—to claim it. The dog was wearing a thick, stark white collar, and the fur of its coat was extremely well-oiled and shiny. It was standing almost as if at attention on all fours, tail and pointed snout both raised and still, eyes staring deeply down into Rev.

Rev. was, to his core, afraid of the dog. But as they stood there, drawn into each other, something in its moist, brown eyes was quite clearly, oddly, peace-filled—and full of an empathy and compassion for Rev. Yet, too, he felt—saw—a fullness of intent all about the animal, a strong-spiritedness with a defined purpose. So he kept still for a moment, continuing to regard it, as it regarded him.

Rev. decided, after a few panting moments, to begin to raise his other foot slowly, to have it join its mate on the same stair. But, as he did so, the dog sharply barked—loudly, and once—staring at him keenly, steadily. Rev. waited a few beats, and tried to lift the leg yet again—but this time, the dog walked further forward toward him, and in his spirit, he felt a force, something saying to him *done done done done done done done*. Frightened, he began slipping back down the stairs backwards—step after step in a quick-slow rhythm unsteadily, eyes always up and on the dog. The dog walked closer to the railing slats, cocking his head to one side, observing Rev. as he retreated. The animal was staring down, down, down, into his eyes and fully. And steps-by-steps, it began following the man—all the way down to his wheezing, half-jogging exit, at the ground level.

Inside the little, rented condo unit, Pallavi Victoria stood there for moments upon moments, propped up like a mannequin on big-woman stilts. She was calmer for having been well soothed by an on-his-way Rhys, Oceania's to-be-risen son—but still dazed and part of a hazy, surreal quadrant of real Time. Then head turning, shaking itself into a now, she ventured to look down and across at the shambled, trickle-by-its mouth-congealed, shell of what was once the living Rodney. She stared numbly at its lengthening shadow and the darkening pool of wine near it, as the sun's rays heightened and changed position. And still partially anchored to the faux wood floor, she felt the force of herself, retroactively wishing. She was wishing and wishing and wishing back that, like with Rodney's spirit, and the excruciating pain, under-scars, and thingified concept of Wifey, the

Presence had also taken her husband's broken, empty, and staring out body—and her tattooed memory of it—up with it, and forever, well away.